Once Upon a Fairytale

Whisked away into a world of fantasy and romance...

With these contemporary love stories inspired by enchanting classic fairytales, a happily-ever-after ending is in store for these two gorgeous couples!

Discover Gabrielle and Deacon's story in
Beauty and Her Boss

Could Gabrielle be the one to shed light into Deacon's locked-away heart?

And read Sage and Quentin's story in
Miss White and the Seventh Heir

Quentin is a billionaire with a secret.
When Sage discovers the truth, will it lead to happily-ever-after?

Both available now!

Dear Reader,

Welcome to the second book in the Once Upon a Fairytale duet. Trey and Sage's story is loosely based on another of my favorite fairytales, *Snow White and the Seven Dwarfs*.

When I was little I had these big books of fairytales. I loved to have them read to me while I gazed at the colorful pictures. Back then I never dreamed that someday I'd get to weave my own version of a fairytale. Talk about fun.

Sage White didn't have an idyllic childhood. To say her relationship with her stepmother was bumpy is an understatement. Now Sage understandably has trust issues, so when she ends up the managing editor of *QTR Magazine* and hires a sexy male assistant, there's an adjustment period.

Quentin Thomas "Trey" Rousseau III is the brand-new CEO of *QTR* who has gone undercover in his own company. He is on a mission to make sure the magazine his father chose over Quentin and his mother is finally run out of business, but he doesn't expect his boss to be so beautiful and compelling. Add in a trip to one of the most romantic spots on earth—the French Riviera—and Trey knows that he's in over his head.

I hope you enjoy reading this romantic fairytale.

Happy reading,

Jennifer Faye

Miss White and the Seventh Heir

—

Jennifer Faye

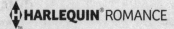

HARLEQUIN ROMANCE

ISBN-13: 978-1-335-13517-9

Miss White and the Seventh Heir

First North American publication 2018

Copyright © 2018 by Jennifer F. Stroka

Award-winning author **Jennifer Faye** pens fun, heartwarming, contemporary romances with rugged cowboys, sexy billionaires and enchanting royalty. Internationally published, with books translated into nine languages, she is a two-time winner of the RT Reviewers' Choice Award. She has also won the CataRomance Reviewers' Choice Award, been named a Top Pick author and been nominated for numerous other awards.

Books by Jennifer Faye

Harlequin Romance

Once Upon a Fairytale

Beauty and Her Boss

Mirraccino Marriages

The Millionaire's Royal Rescue
Married for His Secret Heir

Brides for the Greek Tycoons

The Greek's Ready-Made Wife
The Greek's Nine-Month Surprise

The Vineyards of Calanetti

Return of the Italian Tycoon

The Prince's Christmas Vow
Her Festive Baby Bombshell
Snowbound with an Heiress

Visit the Author Profile page
at Harlequin.com for more titles.

Praise for
Jennifer Faye

"This one had my emotions all over the place. It's funny, tender, heartbreaking...definitely a book you want to read."

—*Goodreads* on *The Greek's Ready-Made Wife*

"Ms. Faye has given her readers an amazing tearjerker with this novel. Her characters are relatable and so well developed...it made everything come to life right off of the page."

—*Harlequin Junkie* on *The Prince's Christmas Vow*

PROLOGUE

ELSA WHITE STOOD before the window of her stylish Manhattan office adorned with black furnishings and gold trim. It wasn't just any office building. It was a skyscraper owned by White Publishing. And Elsa's office was on the top floor. She enjoyed looking down upon the rest of the world.

From her office window, the people below looked like peons—small and inconsequential. She smiled, knowing she was so much better than them. She had money, lots of money, and a powerful reach. She was forever finding ways to make her presence in publishing even greater—legal or illegal, it made no difference to her.

Elsa moved in front of an oversized gold leaf mirror that hung on the wall next to her desk. She pivoted on her black stilettos this way and that way, never taking her gaze off her image. A smile bloomed on her face. Perfect. Her manicured red fingernail slid down over her ivory cheek. There wasn't a wrinkle to be had anywhere on her flawless complexion. Nor should there be with the massive amount she paid her plastic surgeon.

She tucked a few loose strands of platinum-blond hair behind one ear, leaving the other side of her smooth bobbed hair to hang loose. Perfect.

Knock. Knock.

"Come in." She'd told her personal assistant to send in Mr. Hunter, the private detective, as soon as he arrived.

Elsa continued to stare into the mirror. She never tired of her reflection. How could anyone tire of such beauty? Deciding to reapply her "Wicked Red" lipstick, she retrieved the tube of lipstick from the glass table beneath the mirror.

As she removed the cap from the tube, her gaze sought out the man's reflection in the mirror. "Well, don't just stand there. Tell me what you've learned about my stepdaughter."

The tall man with short, dark hair stood his ground, seemingly unfazed by her snappishness. "She's working in Los Angeles."

"So she's still living across the country. Good. Very good." The farther away Sage White remained from Elsa's empire, the better.

"She's working for *QTR Magazine*—"

"What?" Elsa swung around and glared at the man. He never once glanced away or in any way acted as though he was fazed by her anger. This normally would have sparked Elsa's interest, but right now she was preoccupied. "I thought I got her blackballed from all publishing houses."

"You did, but then *QTR* was drawn into some sort of lawsuit and that's how she got her foot in the door. From what I was able to uncover, the senior

Rousseau was forced to step down from the failing company. Before he did so, he put your stepdaughter under an ironclad contract that even the board could not break so long as Miss White showed a steady improvement in the company's profitability."

No longer concerned about her lips, Elsa returned the lipstick to the table. "Why is this the first I'm hearing of it? I pay you good money to keep a close eye on her."

The man's expression hardened. "The deal with *QTR* just happened. They kept everything hush-hush until the contract was signed. Even the board overseeing *QTR* didn't know what had been done until it was too late."

Elsa folded her arms, holding her left elbow up with her right hand. Her long shiny nail tapped on her pointy chin as she considered this new development. She couldn't allow Sage to become successful. With enough funds, Sage could dig into the past. If she were to unearth the truth, she could send the empire that Elsa had lied, deceived and flat-out stolen tumbling into ruin. And that just couldn't happen.

Elsa had outsmarted that girl since the day her father died. She would continue to do so. The company afforded her the lifestyle she deserved and allowed her to maintain her beauty.

Elsa's narrowed gaze zeroed in on Hunter. She had plans for him. "Tell me more about *QTR*."

"It appears they are in a downward spiral. They are losing shelf space in stores and their online presence is shrinking."

"Oh, good. Very good." Her worries diminished, but she knew not to take Sage for granted. She had too much of her father in her. "Keep a close eye on my stepdaughter. She is not to be underestimated. And she cannot be successful at *QTR*. I will stop her at all costs. Now go." Elsa pointed to the door.

The man hesitated as though disliking being ordered around. Elsa was not used to people standing up to her. She liked being able to bend people to her will. She'd never been able to bend Sage and that was why the girl had to go.

When the man turned to the door, Elsa zeroed in on his finer assets—very fine indeed. Perhaps she'd dismissed him too soon. But by then the door was swinging shut. She would have to scratch her itch another time.

Elsa turned back to her reflection. No one was about to unseat her as queen of this publishing empire. She had nothing to worry about—certainly not the likes of that insipid, happy-go-lucky girl. A headline-worthy failure would ruin Sage's future in publishing once and for all.

Elsa broke out in a cackle.

It was all going to work out perfectly. She would see to it.

CHAPTER ONE

Five months later...

SHE ONLY HAD one more month.

One more month to prove that her plan would work—to keep her job.

Sage White worried her bottom lip. Even though she'd stemmed off the hemorrhaging expenses of *QTR Magazine* and in fact was now turning a small profit, she still had a long way to go to appease the board. She had to prove that her plan to reorganize the magazine would work not only now but also for the long term.

The magazine had been on the verge of shutting down when Quentin Rousseau II reached out to her. To say she was surprised by his call was an understatement. She had interned for him in college. He had been wickedly smart and savvy. He took a liking to her. For two summers, she absorbed every bit of knowledge he'd been willing to impart to her. In those days, the magazine still had some integrity. It was in more recent years that fact-checking took a backseat to the sensational headlines.

Quentin Rousseau II had been good to her—he'd even brushed off Elsa's well-planted lies about her. That had not sat well with Elsa, who swore vengeance. The woman's threats hadn't fazed the senior Rousseau. For that, Sage felt indebted to him.

Still, she had been hesitant about accepting the position. Who wanted to step up to the helm of a sinking magazine? However, the elder Rousseau had given her an incentive—a big financial incentive—to make this work. But it also came with a deadline—six months to show improvement and a firm plan for the next year.

Now, sitting behind the managing editor's desk, she wondered if she'd made a mistake. For the last four—almost five—months, she'd spent every waking moment trying to secure the future of the longstanding magazine. With not much more than sheer determination and a skeleton staff, she'd done the impossible—turned the magazine's content one hundred and eighty degrees, from sensationalized headlines to meaningful interviews on important topics. The substantial changes were enough to create a bump in the bottom line. In fact, it impressed the board enough to approve a modest increase in funding. This was making it possible for Sage to at last hire a much-needed PA.

She stared down at the next résumé on her desk. She'd put off hiring a PA as long as possible, not wanting to take funds away from more necessary areas. But with tasks piling up faster than she could tackle them, it was time to hire a very capable, multitasking assistant.

The name on the rather lengthy résumé was Trey Renault. He would be the seventh man in a row that she had interviewed that day. She smiled and shook her head. This definitely wasn't a coincidence.

When she'd casually let it slip that her thirtieth birthday was in a few weeks, Louise, the head of human resources, declared that Sage should find a nice guy to settle down with. Sage tried to politely explain that settling down wasn't on her to-do list. She had a lot of other things that needed her focus. A family would have to wait.

She scrutinized each line of Trey Renault's résumé. His education and references were impeccable. On paper, this man was impressive. But he lacked experience in publishing. Would he be a quick learner?

Her phone buzzed. She answered and learned that the man in question had arrived. She glanced at the time on her desktop monitor and found that he wasn't just five minutes early, he was a full ten minutes early. Oh, a man after her own heart. She told the receptionist to show him back to her office.

Knock. Knock.

Sage stood and smoothed her navy skirt down over her thighs. She then ran a hand over her hair, making sure the long dark strands weren't out of place. She didn't know why she was making such a fuss. It wasn't like she was the one being interviewed.

She came around her desk and opened the door. She had to crane her neck in order to smile up at him. From behind a pair of dark-rimmed glasses his dark gaze met hers, but she was unable to read anything in his eyes. A man of mystery. She was intrigued.

She held out her hand. "Hello. My name's Sage White."

The man's large hand enveloped hers. His grip though firm was not too tight. "*Bonjour.* I am Trey, um… Renault."

A Frenchman. She had to admit, she found his accent sexy. He wasn't so bad himself, in that tall, dark and handsome sort of way. His brown hair was trimmed short on the sides with the top a little longer and a bit wavy. His face was quite attractive, even if it was partially obscured by a full beard and mustache. She couldn't help but wonder what he'd look like after a shave.

"Welcome, Trey." She stepped back to make room for him to enter her office. "Please come in."

His face didn't betray any hint of emotion. Sage closed the door and then turned back to this man who intrigued her more than all the other applicants added together. His gaze moved swiftly around her office as though taking in his surroundings. She wanted to ask what he thought of what she'd done with the space, but she squelched the urge. They had other more urgent matters to discuss.

Once he made his way across the room, he took a seat in one of the two black leather chairs facing her desk. Sage returned to her own chair. She didn't know what it was about this man that had her so intrigued, but there was something different about him aside from the accent—yet there was something familiar, too.

Sage smothered a sigh. She was letting her imagination get the best of her. Trey Renault was an applicant just like the other six bachelors who'd paraded through her office.

The first man she'd interviewed wouldn't so much as shake her hand. He went on to tell her about all of the germs in the world. With his knowledge of illnesses, she started to wonder if he should have gone to medical school and become a doctor.

The second man yawned through the whole interview. She couldn't tell if it was her that had bored him or if he hadn't slept the night before. The third man had definitely woken up on the wrong side of the bed. The scowl on his face seemed to be permanent. He'd complained about everything including his previous employers. The fourth man couldn't stop sneezing. She was beginning to wonder if he was allergic to her.

Bachelor number five was a pleasant change with a nice smile and good attitude, but as the interview went on, she found he'd smile and agree with everything she said. Number six had great looks but it didn't appear he had much going on upstairs.

With the prestigious Cannes Film Festival quickly approaching, which was pivotal to the magazine's future, she had no more time to interview applicants. The truth was they weren't exactly breaking down her door. She had to pick the best of these applicants.

And so far bachelor number seven appeared to be the front runner. Then she caught herself glancing down at his left hand. Yep, another bachelor. Louise had certainly done her homework.

Sage jerked her gaze back up to his handsome face. His chin was squared and his nose straight. But it was his eyes that drew her in with their dark and mesmerizing depths. It'd be so easy to get lost in them. Just like she was doing now.

She jerked her gaze away from him and back to the résumé on her desk. She stared blindly at the paper. With his good looks, he'd definitely make Monday mornings more bearable.

Gathering her thoughts, she welcomed him again. She then started her well-practiced spiel about the highlights of the magazine and an overview of the position requirements. She couldn't be swayed by his good looks. She had a board meeting at the end of the month that would determine her future. And from what she'd heard, her former boss's estranged son had assumed the position of

CEO and he'd made it his mission to put the magazine out of business.

Most people didn't even know this son existed. She'd done an internet search and hadn't been able to come up with even a photo of the mysterious son. In this day and age of social media how was that possible?

His mission was to uncover the truth.

Quentin Thomas Rousseau III had persuaded most of the *QTR* board to do away with his father's beloved magazine. However, his father's last act as CEO had been to install a new managing editor. And somehow this woman—a woman with a questionable past—was turning things around for the business. She was reopening doors with vendors that had previously turned their backs on *QTR Magazine*. She'd eliminated the red ink, and if business kept increasing, she'd soon turn a sizable profit. But how? And why save this sinking ship?

Knowing his father had many connections and lots of money to sway people, the only person Quentin could trust to uncover the truth was himself. However, he couldn't just burst through the doors of *QTR Magazine*, announce that he was the new CEO and expect people to open up to him. It meant he'd have to take extraordinary measures.

And then it'd come to his attention that the new

managing editor was in need of a personal assistant. That was the moment he'd started plotting his fact-finding mission. It was nothing too far out there. After all, there was a reality show about bosses going undercover in their own companies. Why couldn't he do the same thing?

And finally, he needed an alias. He decided to use the name he'd gained in boarding school. His friends thought his real name, Quentin Thomas Rousseau III was just too uppity. He soon became Trey, meaning "the third." His mother had hated it, but he'd liked having a different name than his absentee father. For this mission, he'd combined his nickname with his late mother's maiden name.

Since he'd initially met with the board of QTR International he'd grown a beard and mustache, which he found itchy, and he'd cut his longer hair super short. To finish the look, he'd given up his contacts and purchased dark-framed glasses. Even his own mother would hesitate to recognize him.

His only problem was that he didn't expect Sage White to be so young. He must have missed her age when he'd done his research. And more than that, he didn't expect her to be such a jaw-dropping knockout. The pictures online certainly didn't do her justice. With her dark hair, fair complexion and vivid blue almost violet eyes, he was sorry that they were on opposite sides of this magazine deal—very sorry.

"Mr. Renault?"

There he went letting himself be distracted. He was going to have to work harder to remain focused when he was around her—if he got the job.

"Oui." He cleared his throat. "I mean, yes."

She gave him a strange look and then in a blink it was gone. "I must admit your résumé is quite impressive."

She leaned back in her chair, looking quite at ease as though she were born to sit there. And perhaps she was at ease, considering her father had been a legend in the publishing industry. But something had gone astray after her father's death and somehow Sage White had been blackballed from the industry…until now. What did his father know about Sage White that he didn't?

Sage sent him an expectant look.

"Merci." He'd worked hard to make sure his qualifications would catch her attention. However, the trick was making sure he didn't appear to be overqualified.

She arched a dark brow as she gave him a pointed stare as though she were trying to read his thoughts. "Why would you want to work here at *QTR?*"

To find out about your special brand of magic. And put a stop to it.

Suddenly finding his mouth a bit dry, he cleared his throat. It was best to stick with as much of the truth as possible. "I've heard you're making great strides in turning the magazine around and I would like to be a part of it."

She nodded as though his answer was acceptable. Then she glanced down at his résumé. "I don't see where you have any experience working in the publishing industry."

He'd noticed that, too, when he was putting together his first-ever résumé. He'd never needed one before since he'd started his own software company while still in college. He'd always been his own boss. In fact, he was used to people answering to him, not the other way around. This arrangement was definitely going to take some adjusting for him. But how hard could an assistant position be?

Still, he hadn't wanted his résumé to be too perfect or it would have been suspicious. Nor did he want it to be filled with too much fiction. And so his work experience was limited to positions within a few trusted friends' companies.

Trey swallowed hard. "Publishing is new to me. But I like challenges. And I'm a fast learner."

Again, she nodded. She sat back in her chair and gave him a serious stare. He couldn't help but wonder if she was deep in thought or if she was somehow trying to intimidate him.

"It sounds to me like you get bored easily," Sage said. "Is that the case?"

How had she done that? Read him so easily? He had to admit that it made him a bit uncomfortable. He enjoyed being a man of mystery. "I..." His voice died away as he desperately sought out some answer to assuage her worries. "I thrive on challenges."

The worry that had been reflected in her eyes faded. "I can definitely challenge you."

Suddenly his imagination veered from the subject of business. In his mind's eye, she was challenging him, but it wasn't with reports or emails; instead it was with her glossy full lips. They were so tempting. And the berry-red hue made them stand out against her ivory skin.

He swallowed hard and drew his gaze upward to meet hers. "Then it sounds like we'll make a great team."

"Not so fast. I didn't say you were hired."

"But you will. You need me." He sent her one of his best smiles.

She didn't appear phased. "I don't need anyone."

"So you're one of those."

"What's that supposed to mean?"

Not about to stumble down that rabbit hole, he said, "You need me, you just don't know it yet."

Sage leaned back in her chair and crossed her arms. If she was trying to look intimidating, it wasn't working. "You have a very odd way of interviewing."

He did? That was quite possible, but he'd gained her attention. She wouldn't forget him.

"I'm the man you need. I'm smart, timely and efficient."

"And not lacking in conceit."

He shook his head. "It's not conceit when it's a fact. Give me thirty days and I'll prove it to you."

He could see by the look in her eyes that he was getting through to her. She would hire him. He was certain of that. This interview had lingered longer than he'd ever imagined and she genuinely seemed interested in him—in his skills, that is.

CHAPTER TWO

HE WAS COCKY. She'd definitely give Trey that much.

But sometimes that wasn't such a bad thing.

Sage always did like a challenge. It was his third day on the job and he'd presented a very big challenge. But of all the candidates, he struck her as a get-it-done type. And that's who she needed on her team right now—if she hoped to continue to turn around this magazine.

An email popped up. Sage was just about to call a management meeting, but the subject line caught her attention: *Elsa White*. That name was enough to send her good mood in a downward spiral. What was her stepmother up to this time?

Sage had always known that her stepmother had outmaneuvered her into gaining control of White Publishing. Sage had been young and naive. She'd wanted to believe that her stepmother wasn't a monster, but reality was much harsher than Sage had been prepared to accept at the tender age of eighteen. It had been that particular birthday when she'd lost her childhood home, her destiny and her naivety. She'd been forced to grow up—it came with a lot of painful life lessons.

She knew that if she was wise, she'd let go of the past and keep moving forward, but she couldn't.

She remembered being a little girl and sitting behind her father's large desk at the headquarters of White Publishing. Her father would swing her chair around until she was looking out over the bustling city and he would tell her that one day all of this would be hers. But she was never to take it for granted. As the head of White Publishing, she would have a great responsibility and it went beyond the quarterly results. She needed to be generous, understanding and compassionate with everyone around her.

That had been before he had been bewitched by Elsa. After that, nothing was ever the same. Had her father truly changed his mind about the business and her role in it? It was a question she'd been contemplating off and on for years. Sometimes she thought she knew the answer, and other times she wasn't so sure.

Knock. Knock.

Trey ducked his head inside the door. He looked as though he were going to say something but then he hesitated.

"What did you need?"

"Um…" He stepped farther into the room. "I've sent out that email to the department heads, so I was going to head out to lunch—"

"Already?" She glanced at the time on her computer. A quarter till twelve. She frowned. Did she strike him as some sort of pushover?

"I was in early."

This new role as management was taking some getting used to. For so many years, she'd been the one taking the orders; now she was the one handing them out. But she couldn't let anyone see her discomfort. If she did, she'd lose their respect and it'd be all downhill from there.

"Lunch can wait."

Trey's brows rose. "But I have plans."

"This work needs to be your priority."

Trey opened his mouth, but he immediately closed it.

She grabbed the stack of manila folders from the corner of her desk. In this modern day, they still did a lot of things via hard copy. Going forward, she'd like to automate a number of functions, but for now, like so many other things, it'd have to wait.

Sage held out the files. "I've approved these reports and disbursements. Please see that they get to the appropriate departments."

He stepped forward and accepted the files. "Anything else?"

She refused to let his cool tone get to her. She didn't ask anyone to work any harder than her. "Yes, there is."

And then she began to explain a new report she wanted him to prepare each month analyzing the ad space. Advertising was their bread and butter. She needed to keep a close eye on it and if possible expand the magazine to accommodate a higher frequency and larger campaign. Fashion and cosmetics were their biggest contributors, but she was interested in expanding to other areas such as upscale furniture or designer products.

Trey made notes. "Couldn't you just get this from the advertising department?"

"I could." But she wasn't sure she trusted the supervisor. It was rumored that his work was declining and his lunches were more of the liquid variety. Until she had proof, she was unwilling to act on the rumors.

"Then why don't you?"

She leveled a cold, hard gaze on him. "I asked you to do it, not them."

He at least had the decency to look uncomfortable. "I'll get right on it."

Trey walked away with his tasks in hand. She wondered if she'd handled everything correctly with Trey. She needed to be forceful but not too over the top. Had she pushed too hard?

Second-guessing herself was a bad habit of hers. It was something she'd started to do after her father died and Elsa had found fault with everything Sage did, from the cooking to the cleaning. Sage shoved aside the unhappy memories. There was work to do.

And an email to read.

Sage turned back to her computer monitor and

sighed. For every email she'd responded to that morning, there were two new ones. She worked her way from top to bottom. She assured herself that this was her normal routine and not a stalling tactic, but at last, she opened the email from her private investigator.

The first thing to catch her attention was the fact that the investigator was on to something regarding her stepmother. Thank goodness. He was the third investigator she'd hired. The first had taken her money and produced zero results. The second one had been caught snooping around White Publishing. This third man cost her all of her savings and more. She'd bet everything on him. He was her last hope.

But the second thing to catch her attention was that he needed more money. The sizable retainer she'd previously paid him had given her serious pause. It had wiped out her savings and then some. The only way to pay him more was to get the board's approval of her business plan for the magazine's future and receive the bonus stated in her contract.

Knock. Knock.

At five after twelve, Trey returned. "The paperwork has been dealt with and I have your report started. I'm going to lunch." He studied her for a moment. "Unless that's a problem?"

"That's fine."

"Are you sure? Because you're frowning again."

She nodded. When she saw doubt reflected in his eyes, she said, "Seriously, it's not you. It's an email I received."

"That's what the delete button is good for."

She leaned back in her chair. "You don't know how tempting that is right about now. I have enough headaches. I don't need another one."

"Well, there you go. Problem solved."

"I wish. But deleting the email isn't going to make this problem disappear."

"I take it we're not talking about *QTR*."

She shook her head. "Afraid not. But I can deal with the email later. Go and enjoy your lunch."

"What about you?"

"What about me?"

"It's lunchtime. Remember? You need to take a break and eat."

Was he working his way up to asking her to lunch? The startling realization that she'd enjoy spending a leisurely hour staring across the table at him jarred her. Trey wasn't just any guy. He was her assistant.

She gave herself a mental shake. With the board meeting at the end of the month, she had to stay focused. "I don't have time for lunch today."

"I'm beginning to notice a trend with you."

This was the first personal conversation they'd taken time for since he'd started. The reason she'd chosen him over the other candidates wasn't his dark and mysterious eyes or his potential to be a male cover model. Her reasons were far more basic.

He was smart and cocky—enough so that he'd want to do what it took to make himself stand out in a good way. And that's what she needed. A person ready to hit the ground running. And that's exactly what Trey had done. He'd taken on every task she'd given him—even when it'd kept him here after hours.

She was almost afraid to ask, but she couldn't resist. "What trend would that be?"

"You never have time for lunch or anything else that isn't business related."

Lunchtime was her quiet time. She did eat, but it was always something simple that she could eat at her desk while answering emails and reviewing deadlines.

"It's the way I like it." She'd been working so long and so hard to keep herself afloat that she didn't have time for a personal life. Maybe one of these days when the magazine was back on track and she resolved things with her stepmother. "I need that report completed as soon as you get back."

The truth was she didn't like Trey analyzing her. She didn't want him unearthing her shortcomings. Because aside from his sexy good looks, Trey was astute and not easily won over, which made her want to gain his respect. Did that make her a bad boss? Was she supposed to be immune to the feelings of her employees—even when they were six foot two, physically toned and had mysterious dark eyes?

"Hey, Trey."

Trey nodded and smiled at the passing mail lady. It was the following day and he had yet to complete the advertising report to Sage's satisfaction. Every time he thought he'd nailed it, she changed the criteria. He didn't know if she was trying this hard to make a good impression on the board or if she was trying to make him quit. Either way, she was only delaying the inevitable. Come the end of the month, the board would vote to shut down the magazine.

He honestly never thought when he went undercover that he'd have this much work to do. He thought he'd answer the phone, sort mail and fetch coffee. So far Sage had answered her own phone, the mail provided more projects for his growing to-do list and the boss lady had her own coffeepot. In other words, this job was not the cushy position he thought it'd be.

"Trey, just the person I need to see." Louise, the head of human resources, stood just outside her office door.

He came to a stop. "What do you need?"

"For you to settle a debate." She waved at him to follow her into the office. The older woman with short, styled silver hair sent him a warm smile. Try as he might to remain immune to her friendliness, he liked her.

Something told him this wasn't work related. "I really need to get going. Sage needs this information." He held up the papers in his hand. And for emphasis, he added, "Right now."

Louise shook her head. "Don't worry. This will only take a moment."

He glanced around, finding he wasn't the only one who'd been drawn in. Ron, from subscriptions, was propped against a file cabinet in the corner. He waved and Trey returned the gesture. On the other side was Jane with the short blond hair with pink streaks, but he couldn't recall which department she worked in. She flashed him a big flirty kind of smile. He didn't smile, not wanting to encourage her attention. Instead he gave a brief nod. What in the world had Louise drawn them in here for?

Louise moved to the doorway, checked both directions in the hallway and then proceeded to close the door. She turned to them. "It's come to my attention that Sage's birthday is this month. And I think we should do something for her."

Trey didn't like the sounds of this. He'd come to *QTR* to shut it down, not to make friends. The longer he was here, the harder it was to keep his distance. Just like he knew that Ron loved to surf. He could tell you anything you wanted to know about surfing—even some things you might not care to know. Once Ron started talking, it was hard to get away.

Day by day, the employees of *QTR* were changing from nameless numbers on spreadsheets to smiling faces with families to support. He hadn't factored that in when he'd devised his plan to put his father's cherished company out of business.

And worse yet was Sage's unflagging devotion to saving the magazine. In the little time he'd been here, he'd witnessed her long hours and her attention to details. How was she going to take it when they closed it—when *he* closed it?

"Trey?" Louise's voice drew him from his troubled thoughts.

He glanced up to find everyone staring at him as though expecting an answer. The only problem was he didn't know the question.

As though sensing the problem, Louise held a plate of cookies out to him. "Go ahead. Take one of each. I need to know which to make for Sage's birthday."

He made a point of eating healthy, preferring fruit to desserts. He'd watched his mother drown herself in food after his father abandoned them. His mother's health problems had eventually spiraled out of control. As he waited for her at a doctor's appointment, he swore not to follow in her footsteps.

Still, Louise had made a point of making him feeling welcome at *QTR*. And it wasn't like one cookie was going to hurt anything.

He took the double chocolate cookie with a swirl of white frosting. "But isn't a birthday cake more traditional?"

Louise sent him a knowing smile. "I've already done some investigating and the birthday girl prefers cookies. And since this is her milestone birthday, she can have whatever she prefers."

"Milestone?"

Louise nodded and placed a couple of other flavored cookies in his hand before moving to Jane. "Yes, she's going to be thirty. I couldn't believe it when she'd mentioned it, but I double-checked her personnel file."

Trey had to agree with Louise. His boss didn't look like much more than a college grad, if that. And he was finding it increasingly hard to concentrate on his work with Sage around. Her beauty was stunning. He just wished that she didn't try so hard to micromanage everything—including him.

He made short work of the baked goods, finding them all quite good. In the end, he voted for the double chocolate cookie. Louise beamed as he complimented her culinary skills.

As he walked away, guilt settled on him. He was

about to take jobs away from these people. The *QTR* employees weren't cold and heartless like his father. They were warm, friendly and caring. The exact opposite of his father.

On the way back to his desk more people greeted him with a smile. This was the friendliest office he'd ever been in—even on a Monday morning. It only made him more conflicted about his plan.

CHAPTER THREE

TREY LEANED BACK in his chair, stretched and placed his feet on the corner of his desk. After days of pulling numbers from various sources, the advertising report was officially done—well, at least until Sage gave him yet another adjustment or addition.

Today marked his sixth day on the job and he'd not only completed the report but he'd also managed to cut his workload in half via a combination of macros and a few short computer programs. He was feeling pretty pleased with himself.

He removed the eyeglasses that he hadn't quite adjusted to, closed his eyes and leaned his head back as classic rock music pounded in his earbuds. It was nice to just sit back for a moment and enjoy all that he'd accomplished. After all, he deserved it.

He'd been working nonstop since he'd taken this undercover position. He'd made inroads with the new managing editor, but so far he had yet to uncover her secret to success. Sure she was first in the office and the last one out, but there was more to it. She did keep her office door closed a lot. So what was she up to in there? Were there bribes involved—

His feet were shoved off the desk.

He jerked forward in his seat as his feet hit the floor. His eyes snapped open. Was this someone's idea of a joke? Because it wasn't funny.

And then his gaze met Sage's. Her eyes darkened and appeared almost violet. If it wasn't for the distinct frown on her face, he might have been moved to compliment the striking color of her eyes. But now definitely wasn't the right time.

He straightened up, not sure what to say.

Sage continued to frown as she gestured for him to remove his earbuds.

He'd totally forgotten about them. His full attention had been on his boss. Was it strange that he found her even cuter when she got worked up? Her face flushed. It made him want to pull her into his arms and kiss away her worries. Not that he would ever act on the impulse.

Trey scrambled to pull the earbuds from his ears and then press the pause function on his phone. "What did you need?"

"I've been buzzing you. Didn't you hear?" And then realizing the foolishness of her question, she continued. "There's a red light on your phone. Right here." She pointed it out.

"I was busy."

"Doing what? Taking a nap?"

"Hey, that's not fair. I just finished that report— again. And I needed to rest my eyes for just a moment."

"You finished it?" The frown on her face eased.

He nodded. He reached around her and retrieved the printed and proofed copy from the top of his desk. He still wasn't quite sure of the purpose of this report, but as he handed it over, he noticed Sage's pleased expression.

He hadn't known her long, but in that period of time he'd studied her. She cared a lot about the people that worked for her—except him. They butted heads a lot. He realized that was as much his fault as hers. Thankfully this arrangement wouldn't last too much longer.

He'd also noticed that she held back a lot. Many women he'd dated had been more than willing to share the intimate details of their lives. Not Sage. It wasn't like they were dating. That would never happen. But she never mentioned anything about her life outside these office walls. He found that a bit odd.

"Thank you for this." She started toward her office and then turned back. "From now on, earbuds are prohibited in the office."

He opened his mouth to counter a defense, but the firm line of her glossy lips had him closing his mouth without uttering a word. This was her office—her rules. Even if he didn't see the harm with earbuds. He allowed his employees to use them. His motto was happy workers were productive workers. But the problem was that he wasn't the boss here.

She continued to stare at him. "Aren't you coming?"

"I didn't realize…" His voice trailed off as he scrambled to his feet and followed her.

"I thought you might be interested in the process of deciding on a cover for next week's edition."

She was right. He was definitely interested. Perhaps this was where she sprinkled her fairy dust that made all the vendors sit up and take notice of *QTR* once again. "Yes, I would be very interested."

She gestured for him to follow her into her office. Three large computer monitors sat on a table. She moved to her desktop computer and pressed a couple of keys. Her gaze moved to the monitors, which remained dark. Her fine brows drew together as her rosy lips pursed together. She tried again with the same results.

Computers were his field of expertise. "Can I give it a try?"

She shook her head. "I've got it."

She tried again with the same results.

"I'm pretty good with computers." He moved to her side ready to take over.

He reached for the keyboard at the same time she did. Their fingers touched. Her hand was soft and warm. And her touch sent a wave of attraction washing over his eager body.

When he raised his gaze, he caught the look of desire in Sage's eyes. But in a blink it was gone and he was left wondering if it had ever been there at all.

She glanced away. "I'll get it. Just hang on."

"You do realize that I'm your assistant, right? So let me assist."

"No. I can figure this out."

"Are you always so stubborn?"

Her gaze met his. "I refer to it as independent."

He shook his head and backed off. He wondered what had happened to her to make her so stubborn and unwilling to accept help.

After flipping through a couple of papers and reading something, she tried again. A triumphant smile lit up her face as the monitors flickered on. "There we go. I hit the wrong key before."

Each monitor displayed a cover of *QTR*. There were different headlines and different fonts. He had to admit that this was all new to him as for so much of his career he'd focused on software development and website design.

"These are the three layouts that my staff has put together for the upcoming week." She gave him a moment to read the headlines. "Now they want me to choose which will have the biggest reach both online and in the supermarket aisles."

He read each headline.

Superstars Go Pink and Blue
Serenaded Beneath the Stars
Singing for Angels

Trey turned to Sage. "They're each different stories?"

"No."

He frowned. He hoped she wasn't going to slip into his father's old ways. Had she decided that responsible journalism was just too hard? Disappointment hit him. He'd expected so much more from her.

He crossed his arms. "Is this a bit of sensational journalism? A tricky headline to draw in the reader and then a story that takes enormous liberties with the facts of the story—"

"Certainly not." She studied him for a moment. "I was hired to put integrity back into this magazine and that's exactly what I intend to do."

"So there's a country superstar in the backwoods?"

"Something like that. There's a charity event in San Diego to fundraise for the children's ward in a local hospital. There's a lineup of celebrity singers from pop to classic to country. The benefit concert will be televised and have a very special audience. The children in the hospital that are well enough will be moved by wheelchair to the outdoor garden area. Others will see it televised live in their rooms and they will also meet some of the performers afterward."

He breathed easier knowing that she hadn't resorted to nefarious means of keeping the magazine afloat. And then it struck him that he was rooting for her. When had that happened?

He gave himself a mental shake. She was getting inside his head with her pretty smile and her good heart. But he couldn't let himself get caught up in her plans as he had his own job to do.

"What do you think?" Her voice jarred him from his thoughts.

"It sounds like it will be a successful event."

"It will. The tickets are all sold out."

"I'm assuming you got a couple." He wouldn't mind helping such a good cause. He could accompany Sage—unless she already had a date. The thought didn't sit well with him.

"I did." She gave him a strange look. "Is something wrong?"

He shook his head, hoping it would chase away the unwanted thoughts. "No. Will you, ah, need someone to accompany you?"

"The tickets aren't for me. I've assigned a reporter and a photographer."

For some reason that he didn't want to examine too closely, her answer disappointed him. He would have liked getting to know Sage outside of the office. She was a complex person. She had a good heart, but she didn't let people get too close. She was willing to help people, but she refused to be helped. The more he got to know her, the more he wanted to know about her.

Sage stared at the three layouts. "Does one speak to you more than the others?"

"The singing for angels one makes me want to know who is singing and are they really singing to angels."

"My thought exactly." She turned off the other layouts and focused on the one he'd suggested. "I think the headline should be larger."

"Aren't you going to run a photo to go with the headline?"

"No."

"I think you should."

"That's what other publications would do."

"They do it because it works."

Her gaze narrowed in on him. "Are you saying you don't trust my judgment?"

"I'm saying why take chances when a photo will draw the fans?"

She leaned a curvy hip against her desk. "And what about the readers that aren't big fans of the celebrity? Will they be drawn in, too?"

He shrugged. He hadn't considered that angle. "But what if no one picks up the magazine or opens the digital edition?"

"Nothing is guaranteed."

"Then why take a risk?" He stopped himself, realizing that by playing devil's advocate he was fighting for the magazine to succeed. What was it about being around Sage that mixed up his thoughts?

"Because it's my call." Her tone was firm.

He got the hint. She was the boss and he wasn't. So his opinion didn't count. This gave him pause.

He'd said similar words to his own employees. He hadn't any idea of how those words felt when you were on the receiving end. Going forward, he'd have to listen more and let his employees know that he valued their opinion.

"You've heard things about me, haven't you?" Her gaze met his straight-on. Not giving him a chance to answer, she continued. "I know people talk, but if you think I'm going to let this magazine fold, you've been talking to the wrong people. I know what I'm doing."

Suddenly he realized her response had less to do with him and more to do with her proving herself. The look in her eyes said the opposite of her words. In her blue eyes, he saw worry and doubt.

What was it about him that got to her?

Sage sat at her desk that evening. It was well past quitting time, but she had emails she'd pushed off all day that needed responses.

Besides, even if she went home, she wouldn't be

able to rest. Her mind kept replaying her disagreement with Trey. For some reason, he got under her skin. And that wasn't good. She couldn't afford to be distracted.

He was still in his ninety-day trial period. Letting him go at this stage would be quick and painless.

Tap. Tap.

Sage glanced up to find Louise standing in the open doorway. "I thought I'd find you here."

"Am I that predictable?"

Louise nodded. "You need a life beyond these office walls."

She would, just as soon as she reclaimed the legacy that Elsa stole from her. Until then, she had to keep working at *QTR* and earn her bonus in order to pay the private investigator. Someday this all would end.

"You looked like you had something serious on your mind when I walked in." Louise took a seat. "Anything you want to talk about?"

"It's Trey. I'm not sure he's going to work out."

"Really?" There was genuine surprise in Louise's voice. "I thought he was easy on the eyes."

He was. That was one of the problems. And when his hand had lingered on hers, her stomach had dipped like she was riding a roller coaster.

"He, um…doesn't do things the way I expect them to be done."

"But he does them?"

Sage grudgingly nodded. "And he has this habit of disagreeing with me."

"So you want someone who agrees with everything you say?"

"No, but he's..."

"He's what?"

Distracting her—making her think of her sorely lacking social life. "He's still on probation and I just want to make sure he's the right fit."

"As shorthanded as you are, can you afford to be picky?"

Louise was right. The Cannes Film Festival was later that month, and if they were fortunate enough to get passes, she needed someone reliable to help with it. And on top of being sexy, Trey had proven he was reliable.

She sighed. "You're right. There isn't time to find a replacement."

"I think he'll surprise you."

That's what she was afraid of.

His feet pounded the asphalt.

His muscles burned in that satisfying way.

His lungs strained to pull in more oxygen.

And Trey never felt more alive than when he was pushing his body to the limit. He normally made a point of running every morning. Today wasn't normal. His life was anything but normal since he met Sage.

With evening setting in, he continued running—pushing himself. After bumping heads with Sage most of the afternoon, he was filled with pent-up energy. That woman was so frustrating and yet so enticing. He couldn't decide whether he wanted to yell at her or pull her into his arms and kiss her.

He let out a frustrated groan as he slowed to a walk a block from his condo. The sooner he got the information he'd come to *QTR* for, the better. Ever since he'd stepped inside the office, everything had grown increasingly complicated.

The shrubbery next to him shook. He came to a stop. There was no wind to explain the sudden rush of motion. It was probably a squirrel. He was about to move on when he heard a high-pitched whine. Or was it a bark. Could there be a dog in there?

Trey peered closer at the bush. In the long shadows of evening, it was hard to make out a dog in between the leafy limbs. Then the bush moved again.

Arf! Arf!

Trey straightened and looked around to see if someone was looking for their dog. The bush was sitting next to a park, but no one was around. Just then a car turned onto the street. By the time it reached Trey, it was well above the speed limit. He didn't want anything to happen to the dog.

Trey turned back to the bush. Why was the dog

in the bush? Had it gotten lose from its leash and gotten scared?

Trey already had enough of his own problems. He didn't need someone else's. But if he had lost a pet, he would want someone to go out of their way and make sure it got safely home.

With a sigh because he knew that he wasn't going to get anything else done that evening, he crouched down next to the bush. "Come here, fella. It's okay. I won't hurt you."

Arf! Arf!

The bark had to be a positive sign, right? Trey hadn't had a dog growing up. His mother said that she had her hands full with him and running the house alone. She couldn't take on a dog, too. As such, he didn't really know much about animals.

He kept his voice soft. "Come on. Come here."

He kept talking to the dog in gentle tones, hoping the dog would trust him enough to poke its head out. He wished that he had some food on him. If worse came to worst, he could run home and grab some food—

The leaves moved again. A little head poked out.

Trey didn't waste any time. He cautiously moved his fisted hand toward the dog, hoping it wouldn't bite him. Instead it sniffed him.

"Good boy." Trey made sure to keep his voice low and steady. "I'm going to pick you up, but you don't have to worry. I won't hurt you. Promise."

And then he swiftly reached into the bush and wrapped his hand around the dog's midsection. A clipped bark signaled the dog's surprise. Before the dog could move, Trey was lifting it to him.

The dog weighed practically nothing. In fact, he could feel the dog's ribs. Its fur was matted and dirty. Sympathy welled up in Trey.

"What in the world has happened to you?"

The dog shook with nerves. Ignoring the filth, Trey pulled the dog against his chest, trying to comfort it. The dog didn't fight him. Trey wondered if it was because the dog at last knew it was safe or if it just didn't have the strength to fight.

"Come on, buddy. Let's get you home and fed."

Trey felt awful that he'd almost kept going. The little dog was desperate for someone to care for it. He didn't know that he was the ideal person for the job, but he would do his best.

CHAPTER FOUR

THE NEXT MORNING, Sage kept checking Trey's outer office. Usually he arrived early, but not today. She checked the time. He still had another fifteen minutes. Why did he have to pick today of all days to sleep late? She had big news to share with him.

After speaking with Louise, she decided that between the exhaustion and the stress, she'd blown that hand-touching episode out of proportion. After all, he arrived at work every day and was never late. He got his work done. What more did she want?

She knew what else was bothering her. This attraction that was arcing just beneath the surface could be a problem when it was just the two of them on the very romantic French Riviera. And this upcoming business trip couldn't be canceled. The future of *QTR Magazine* was riding on it.

She'd just learned that her request for passes to the Cannes Film Festival had been approved. The committee had honored the magazine's long-standing attendance and granted them three passes. One for the photographer and two for people to cover it with interviews.

She would need Trey's help on this trip. The thought of covering the Cannes Film Festival on her own seemed, well, quite overwhelming.

Sage was hoping to make inroads with more stars and perhaps cover more than just their appearance at the festival. She had learned quickly that turning this magazine around was all about making contacts, whether it was a distributor, vendor or A-list actor. It was all about who you knew. And quite frankly, she'd exhausted her very short list of famous acquaintances.

She had just taken a seat at her desk to respond to some emails when she heard a noise. It sounded like Trey. Anxious to finalize the plans, she headed for the door.

"I've been waiting for you. I have news." She stopped in her tracks. A ball of white fur was sticking out from under Trey's arm. "What is that?"

He turned to her. His hair was scattered. His shirt was unbuttoned at the collar and his tie was stuffed in his pocket. "It's more like who is this?"

She frowned at him. "I'm not playing games. Is that a dog?"

Trey nodded. "I can explain—"

"You can't have a dog in here."

"I didn't have a choice."

"You should have left him at home." She glanced around, hoping no one else was nearby. She didn't need everyone thinking that it was all right to bring their pet to work. "Come in my office."

Once they were both…er…all three in the office, she closed the door. This was not the smooth start to the day that she'd been hoping for. And after Louise had soothed her worries about keeping Trey on staff, he pulled this stunt.

"Listen, I know this is awkward." The dog began to wiggle in his arms. "Do you mind if I put him down?"

Sage shook her head. It probably wasn't a wise decision. What if it peed on the carpet? Or worse?

Trey set the white dog on the carpet. She was relieved to see that the dog had a collar and leash. He began to sniff around, taking in his new surroundings. Sage kept an eye on it. She told herself that it was to make sure it didn't make a mess and not because it was the most adorable ball of fluff. When it stopped in front of her and turned those big brown eyes on her, she longed to pick it up and cuddle him. But she just couldn't give in to that temptation. She was the boss. She had to set an example.

She forced her gaze away from the cute pup and back to her assistant. "I don't know what you were thinking by bringing him here, but he has to go. Now. And preferably without anyone seeing you."

"But that's the problem. I don't have anywhere to take him."

"I'd think taking him home would be an ideal solution."

"But he's not mine."

Before she could speak, she felt something cold

and wet against her leg. She glanced down to find the dog sniffing her. Her instinct was to kneel down and make friends, but she didn't want Trey to think that whatever he was trying to pull here was acceptable. This was one of those moments when she didn't like being management.

Sage turned her attention back to Trey. "Do you normally bring other people's animals to work with you?"

"I must admit that it's a first."

"And your last."

"If you would let me finish. I can explain this. It's really kind of a funny story." He hesitated. "Actually, it's not funny ha-ha. It's funny as in strange and a bit sad."

She should be upset, but when the puppy looked at her with those big innocent eyes, her irritation melted away. The little white dog with long fur was so cute. No wonder Trey had taken it in.

Unable to resist any longer, she asked, "Can I pet him?"

"Um, sure." Trey's face filled with confusion soon followed with relief. "He's a very friendly little guy."

"Hi." She knelt down and pet him. His white fur was soft, but it was long and gnarled. "You are such a sweet thing. That's great that you adopted a dog—"

"I didn't adopt him. It's more like he adopted me."

Sage straightened. "Say again."

The dog moved and sat at Trey's feet. Its little tail swished back and forth. "I found him hiding in a bush when I was out running last night. He was shaking with fear."

"Aw...poor baby?"

Trey nodded. "He didn't have a collar or any way to identify him. And from the looks of him, no one has cared for him in quite a while. I took him home, fed him and cleaned him up the best I could."

"There's one thing I don't understand. Why did you bring him to work?"

"I didn't mean to. I thought the animal shelter would be open early, but it opens late today. If I could just keep him here until they open—"

"You aren't keeping him?" She glanced down at the little dog that was now leaning up against Trey's leg as though they belonged together. "He seems to have really bonded with you."

"I... I'm not a dog person."

She arched a brow. "Really? Because you certainly seem like it to me and...what do you call him?"

"I didn't name him because I'm not keeping him."

"You can't keep calling him puppy or dog." She turned her attention back to the white puppy. "Come here."

Surprisingly, the dog came right to her. It's little

tail swished back and forth. "You certainly are a friendly little guy."

"He's certainly that. Even when he woke me up at 4:00 a.m. to take him outside. He was as happy as could be. Me not so much. I was half-asleep and almost walked into the wall."

She scooped the dog up in her arms. "Is that true? Are you a happy little guy?"

Arf!

Sage couldn't help but smile at the dog's cheery personality.

"Maybe you should keep him," Trey suggested.

"Me? I don't think so. I spend all of my time here at the office." She couldn't resist running her hand over the dog. It was when she touched his front leg that it whimpered. "Is it hurt?"

Trey frowned. "Not that I know of. But he was so dirty last night that I might have missed something when I was cleaning him up."

Sage moved to her desk and set the dog down. "He whimpered when I touched his front right leg."

They worked together until they uncovered a nasty, oozing cut beneath some knotted fur. Sage scooped the dog back in her arms, careful not to touch the wounded area. Through it all, the pup continued to wag its tail.

Trey reached out to pet him. "You certainly are one happy guy."

"That's it."

"What's it?" Trey looked utterly confused.

"His name. We'll call him Happy."

"Really?" Trey's gaze moved from Sage to the dog, whose tail picked up speed. "I guess it fits." Staring at the dog, he asked, "Would you like the name Happy?"

Arf! Arf!

Sage laughed. "I think he agrees."

"I'll take him over to the shelter. I'm sure they'll know what to do with him."

Sage looked into Happy's eyes and she just couldn't let him go to some shelter where he would get lost in the crowd and possibly forgotten about. She had to be sure that he was well taken care of.

"Call the Smith Veterinarian Clinic. Tell them you found a stray and its injured. If they give you any problems, you can mention my name. It might help."

He sent her a puzzled look. "I thought you said you didn't have time for pets."

Busted. "I don't have any pets. But that doesn't mean that I don't have roommates with pets."

Trey's eyes widened and he smiled as though his problems were solved.

"Don't," she warned. "I'm not keeping him. But I want to make sure that he's taken care of. Besides, as I recall, you're the one that found him."

"Okay. Okay. I'll call."

Knock. Knock.

The door opened and Louise stuck her head inside. "Good morning. I..." Louise's voice faded away as she took in the sight of Trey's disheveled look. "Sorry. I just wanted to tell you about some new coffee I picked up last night. But it can wait."

Arf! Arf-arf!

Louise's gaze lowered to the floor. "Well, who are you?"

Arf! Arf!

Everyone chuckled at the dog's response.

"And you're a chatty one, too." Louise walked farther into the room.

Sage turned to Trey. "I've got the dog. Go make the call. Tell them it's an emergency and we're on our way."

"We?"

"Yes. Now hurry up."

Her father always told her that if you wanted something done right to do it yourself. It was a philosophy that she'd taken to heart, much like her approach to fixing *QTR*. And she wouldn't get any work done until she was certain Happy was on the mend.

She impressed him.

And that wasn't an easy thing to do.

Trey couldn't believe how Sage had set aside her work and worried over the pup until it had a proper bath, trim, stitches and antibiotics. Not necessarily in that order. During the examination, the vet had revealed that the dog was chipped. And all of his shots were up to date.

And now as they sat in the car, an awkward silence enveloped them. Trey needed a distraction from thinking about what they were attempting to do—return Happy to the owner that had lost him. And as far as he could tell, the owner hadn't searched for him—at least, not for long.

As he slowed for a stop sign, he chanced a quick glance at Sage. She was fussing over the dog. The dog looked perfectly contented and none the worse for wear after his veterinarian appointment. Either that dog was the most laid-back animal or Sage had a magical touch.

"Did you have pets growing up?" Trey returned his attention to the road.

"I did. All sorts of pets. My father enjoyed indulging me."

"What sort of pets?"

"I had a white-and-black cat named Mittens. And I had a couple of birds—"

"Wait." He slowed for another stop sign. "Are you saying you had a cat and birds at the same time?"

She smiled and nodded.

"But how? Aren't cats supposed to hunt birds?"

"Not Mittens. She found them interesting for about five minutes but then she went on her way."

"Amazing." He shook his head in disbelief. "I take it you're good with animals."

She shrugged. "I had a rat. He didn't like me much. He bit me and hid in his cage."

Trey laughed. "You had a pet rat?"

"What's so funny about that?" she asked with a perfectly straight face.

He subdued his amusement. "Nothing. It's just that you never cease to surprise me."

"I also had fish, a bunny—" she paused as though to think about it "—a hamster and a guinea pig."

"You had a very interesting childhood."

He didn't want to stop driving. This was the first time Sage had let down her guard with him and he liked it. She was a lot different outside the office—more relaxed and much more approachable.

"It was amazing." There was lightness to her voice as she drew upon her memories. "For my birthday, my father didn't get me presents. He said that I got enough throughout the year. Instead he would take me on an adventure. We would visit a different part of the world each year. Those are some of my very best memories. We would explore new cultures and the food—it was amazing. My father told me I didn't have to eat it all, but I did have to sample a little of everything. I was surprised by some of the cuisine that I enjoyed—especially my first experience with sushi."

"Your father sounds like he was a really great guy. You must have loved him a lot." A stab of jealousy dug into Trey. He'd never had a relationship like that with his father.

"I did. My father was the best. He did everything he could to give me a great childhood. The only thing that would have made it better is if my mother had been able to share those experiences with us. But she...she died when I was just a baby."

"I'm sorry you lost her. But I'm sure she's smiling down on you."

"Me, too." Sage lowered her voice. "Sometimes I talk to her. Do you think that's silly?"

Without hesitation, he shook his head. "Everyone needs to talk to their mum now and then."

Sage nodded. "Between my father and my pets, I felt truly loved."

Trey envied her childhood. His was quite different. His mother might have been there physically, but she was quiet and withdrawn after his father left. Trey always wondered if a part of her had died when his father abandoned them.

"You don't want to do this, do you?" Sage asked, interrupting his thoughts.

"Do what? Take Happy back to his owner? The same owner that let him loose and didn't even put up posters for his return or post any sort of notice online—"

"How do you know that they didn't? Did you look?"

He could feel her intense stare as he maneuvered the car down the street. "I might have done a quick search last night while Happy was getting adjusted to his new surroundings."

"I bet you did more than a quick search."

Was she able to read him that easily? He wondered what she made of him. He was tempted to ask, to see how much she got right. The question hovered on the tip of his tongue.

"Stop!"

There was nothing in front of them. He checked the rearview mirror as he jammed the breaks. "What's the matter?"

"This is it."

"What is?"

She pointed out the window at the older home with the front door hanging open and a moving truck in the driveway. Beside the driveway was a wrought-iron post with the street number. Sage was right. This was the place. He'd been so caught up in his thoughts that he'd almost passed it by.

He wheeled the car into a parking spot on the street. He glanced out Sage's window at the stately home. Not too big, but not small either. The outside was stone and the front door was red and arched. The hedges were trimmed. And a for-sale sign was in the front yard.

Arf! Arf!

"Sounds like Happy knows he's home." Sage didn't smile.

So all it took was a cute dog to win her over. He was beginning to wonder if Sage was having second thoughts about returning the dog. All he had to say was the owner better have an explanation for letting the dog loose and not searching for him. It better be a really good excuse.

"Okay. Let's get this over with." Trey exited the car and quickly made his way around to open Sage's door.

Happy was so excited and wiggly that Sage let him down. With his leash on, he led them across the road and up the walk to the open front door. Trey wasn't happy about this. He didn't want to see anything else happen to Happy. The little dog could have died out on the streets. And where was his owner? Moving away without their dog?

Trey was about to ring the buzzer when an older man with gray hair entered the foyer with a big box in his hands. His eyes widened when he saw them standing on the landing. "If you came to look at the house, it's by appointment only."

Didn't the man see the dog? Didn't he care? Trey struggled to keep his temper in check. "We didn't come to look at the house."

As though Sage could tell that Trey wasn't at all pleased with any of this, she said, "We came because we…er…rather *he*—" she gestured to Trey "—found your dog."

"My dog? I don't have one."

Sage bent over and scooped up Happy. "You mean, this isn't your dog?"

Happy licked her cheek and wagged his tail. Trey wondered what it was like to be that happy, even after the one person who was supposed to love and protect you disappears from your life. Trey was not the least bit happy.

"That's my mother's dog." The man set the box down and came closer. "I didn't know what had happened to him. I thought the people who were supposed to be taking care of him for her had taken him home."

"No." Trey wasn't happy with the man's lack of concern. "He's been wandering the streets half-starved and injured."

The man's hesitant gaze met his before it turned back to the dog. He reached out to pet Happy and a low growl filled the air. Both Trey and Sage turned surprised gazes at the dog. He seemed to like everyone except this man.

"Is your mother home?" Sage asked.

The man shook his head, making his comb-over slide down on his forehead. With a swipe of his hand, it moved back over the bald spot. "She passed on last week."

"Oh. I'm so sorry." Sage looked a bit awkward as though not sure what to say next.

"Will you be taking care of the dog?" Trey asked, not sure the man would do any better than the dog-sitter who originally lost Happy.

The man's brows drew together. "I can't. My apartment doesn't allow pets. And...and as you can see, that dog has never liked me."

Trey trusted Happy's judgment of people. After all, the dog was crazy about Sage. But how could he not be with the way she fussed over him?

"Are you sure?" Sage asked. "He's a really well-trained dog."

"Trust me. He wouldn't be happy with me."

Trey didn't need any reassurances from the man. It was obvious Happy didn't belong with him. "We're sorry for your loss. We'll be going."

Trey placed a hand on Sage's elbow and turned back toward the car.

"What about the dog?" the man asked.

"We'll take care of him," Sage replied with certainty. "Don't worry. He'll have a good home."

And with that they made their way back to the car.

Once they were both inside and driving away, Trey glanced at Happy contentedly lying in Sage's lap with his chin resting on her knee. "Did you really mean that? You know, about us taking care of Happy?"

She shrugged. "It wasn't like we could leave him with that man. Did you hear the way Happy growled at him?"

"Yeah. He sure didn't like the guy. Wonder what he did to the dog."

"I don't want to know. I just want to make sure that Happy is safe."

"Should we take him to the shelter?"

"We can't do that," she said quickly. "You know, because of his stitches. We need to keep an eye on him and make sure it doesn't get infected."

Trey nodded as though he understood, but he didn't. Not really. He was certain there were skilled people at the shelter that could care for Happy, but he didn't say anything. It appeared Happy had won Sage's heart.

Sage had a way of casting a magical spell over the males in her orbit. If Trey wasn't careful, he was going to forget about his real reason for working at *QTR*. And he just might give in to his desire to kiss her.

CHAPTER FIVE

IT IS NO big deal. After all, it is only temporary.

The excuses crowded into Sage's mind as she made a spot for Happy on the couch in her office. It wasn't like they could trust just anyone to make sure Happy didn't chew his stitches. Thankfully he wouldn't have them in very long. And hopefully there would be no need for the cone the vet had sent along with them—just in case.

Happy put his head down between his paws and his eyes drifted closed. He'd had a big day and it was only lunchtime. Trey had volunteered to run downstairs to the restaurant and grab them some food. In this instance, she wouldn't make a fuss over the restaurant's exorbitant prices. That way they could have a working lunch and make up for some of the time they'd missed that morning as well as keep an eye on Happy.

As it was, she still had big news to share with Trey. And this adventure with Happy had shown her a different side of him. She'd admired the way he'd not only taken in a stray dog but also cleaned him up, bought supplies and cared enough to risk bringing him to the office.

Trey cared a lot more for Happy than he was willing to let on. She noticed how he asked the vet all sorts of questions. And then again when he grew protective when they attempted to take Happy home.

As though sensing that she was thinking of him, Trey breezed through the doorway. He smiled at her. "I picked something a little different."

She made a point of having a salad every day for lunch. "What did you pick?"

"Quit looking so worried. I think you'll approve." And then, as though he wasn't so sure, he added, "And if you don't, I'll get you a chicken salad."

She smiled. If she ever thought of having a family, she would want someone like Trey. He was sweet and thoughtful but not afraid to push boundaries when the need arose. He definitely would make some woman a good husband. She could imagine him with a baby in his arms.

She gasped. What in the world had gotten into her? He was her assistant. Not boyfriend material. No matter how attractive she might find him. She had to keep these wayward thoughts at bay. Maybe all the long lonely nights at the office were catching up with her.

"What's the matter?" Trey stared at her. The concern was written all over his face. "Is it Happy?"

"No. He's fine." She swallowed down her discomfort. "Why do you think something is wrong?"

"You gasped."

Oh, yes, that. Hmm... "I just remembered that I have something important to discuss with you and we're running out of time."

He continued to stare at her as though not sure if he believed her or not. Even Happy had lifted his head and was staring at her. She was going to have to work harder at keeping her thoughts in line. And if she did have an errant thought, she would not—could not—react.

"Are you going to serve up that mystery food? I'm starving." She cleared off space on her desk so they could eat there.

Trey quickly served up the food. When he lifted the lid on hers, he said, "It's citrus grilled salmon with rice noodles and vegetables."

She was quite pleased with the selection. "But how did you know that I love salmon?"

He retrieved his lunch from the bag. "Truth?"

She nodded, wondering if Louise had been his source of information. If so, she was going to have to say something. She couldn't have Louise going around sharing all her personal information—no matter how well intended.

"I guessed." He sent her a smile. She refused to acknowledge the way the twinkle in his eyes made her stomach dip.

"Good guess."

"And how's—" Trey nodded toward Happy "—he doing?"

"You wouldn't even know he didn't belong here all along. He's made himself right at home."

"You know the longer he's here, the harder it's going to be to give him up."

She didn't want to think about parting with the dog. "How about we cross that bridge when we get to it?"

Trey looked as though he were going to say something else, but then he nodded in agreement.

After they were halfway through their meal, Sage glanced over the glass desktop at him. "Is your passport up to date?"

His brows rose high on his forehead. "It is."

"Good. I have exciting news. We're attending the Cannes Film Festival."

The lack of expression on his face surprised her. "And you're looking for an escort?"

He didn't have any idea just how appealing that sounded to her. In fact, it surprised her quite a bit. She prided herself on being self-sufficient and not needing someone in her life. After her father's funeral, she'd felt profoundly alone. She'd foolishly thought Elsa would feel the same way and that they could lean on each other. She couldn't have been more wrong.

Her stepmother had taught her that the only person Sage could count on was herself. Being reduced to Elsa's maid after her father's death had been jarring, but then to be kicked out of her childhood home on her eighteenth birthday drove home that lesson. Sage had never felt more alone—more betrayed.

And it reminded her not to get too comfortable with Trey. They'd shared a moment of friendship today as they helped Happy, but it needed to stop.

"Sage? Hey. Hello." Trey waved his hand in front of her face. When she focused in on him, he asked, "Where did you go?"

"Sorry. I just got lost in my thoughts."

"Not happy ones, I take it."

"Was it that obvious?" She really didn't have a poker face.

He nodded. "If you don't want me to go to France with you, I'm fine with that."

"No, it's not that. I was just thinking about my stepmother."

"Thinking about going to France with me makes you think of your stepmother? I'm confused."

Sage shook her head. "Don't mind me. I guess I'm just tired. But in answer to your question, no, I don't need an escort. I do, however, need an assistant to stay on top of things both here and there."

He hesitated.

"Is that going to be a problem?"

He shook his head. "I can handle it."

"Good. We need to find out which Hollywood stars plan to be in attendance and then we have to research what's going on in their world that they might want to talk about—a new house, a vacation, an upcoming film project or a charity. Or whatever is of interest to them."

"So you want to provide a platform for the stars to share with the world something of their choice."

"Exactly. If the celebrity is excited about a subject, it will come across in the article and hopefully the readers will get excited, too."

"And you plan to do all these interviews at the festival?"

She shook her head. "As nice as that would be, it's not practical. We're going to be there to generate connections and set up interviews for a later date."

He stared at her for a moment. "Is that how you've gotten all of those interviews that have changed the entire platform of the magazine?"

"You read them?"

He paused as though considering his answer. "After our interview, I wanted to make sure I was on top of things. So I read a bunch of back issues."

"Including the scuzzy ones that got the senior Rousseau in trouble?"

He nodded. "What exactly happened there?"

She knew some of it and had pieced together other parts, but she wasn't in a position to reveal details. "It was the board's decision to change the direction of the magazine."

He arched a dark brow as though hoping for more information.

"Don't look at me like that. I can only say so much."

"Fair enough." He took another bite of food. A few moments later, he said, "And this trip, it's important to you?"

"It is."

He nodded. "It's been a while since I've been back to France."

"I take it you grew up there."

"I did, but then I moved away."

"You mean for work?"

"Yeah. Something like that."

So she wasn't the only one holding things back. The part that surprised her was that she wanted to know more about him. She wanted to know everything about him. Maybe this trip to a romantic, seaside town wasn't such a good idea, after all. But it was too late to back out. She truly needed the help. And to tell him that he would no longer be accompanying her would only arouse his curiosity.

He was going home.

Trey worked hard to mask an emotional response. He'd had the house closed up after his mother passed away. He'd moved his business to the States—San Francisco to be exact. But to go home again, it filled him with a rush of conflicting emotions.

And when he did go back—when he faced those painful memories—he didn't want an audience. He wanted to do it on his terms.

"You don't look happy about this opportunity." Sage took a bite of her lunch.

His gaze met her puzzled look. "It's great." He searched for a way out. After all, there were other employees who could accompany Sage. "When did you say we'd be leaving?"

"I didn't. We don't have plane reservations yet. I was hoping you could work on it."

His thoughts immediately turned to the private jet he'd recently acquired. With it, there wouldn't be any problems flying whenever they wanted to. But that was another part of himself that he couldn't share.

"I'll work on it. What day would you prefer?"

"The festival begins next Wednesday." She glanced at her day planner. "I'd say Monday. Tuesday at the latest."

He made a note on his phone.

Just then Happy woke up. He sat up on the end of the couch. He yawned and then shook his head.

Sage smiled. "Looks like someone had a good nap."

Happy jumped down and with his tail wagging ran over to Trey.

"Hey, boy." He pet him. "Looks like you're starting to feel better." Trey lifted his gaze to meet Sage's. "Thanks for letting him stay here with us."

"What's the point of being the boss if you can't bend the rules every now and then?" As though Happy sensed she was talking about him, he moved around the desk to visit her. "But of course when you're all better, you'll have to stay home."

Arf!

Trey laughed. "I don't think he agrees."

And then a thought came to him—a way to get out of traveling with his beautiful boss, who made him forget his mission and made him long to take their relationship to a much more personal level.

Trey cleared his throat. "I really should stay here with Happy. With his condition—" which wasn't that serious but it could have been "—Happy shouldn't be left alone."

"Does someone need a babysitter?" A familiar voice came from the doorway.

They both turned to the door to find Louise standing there with a stack of files in her arm and a smile on her face. Happy ran over to her. His tail moved so fast that it was nothing more than a blur of motion. Louise knelt down and fussed over the dog. He stood up, pressed his paws to her knee and licked her cheek.

"I think the answer to your problem just walked in the door." Sage smiled at Happy's antics.

The dog sure had won over Sage. He hadn't had

as much luck with Sage. The woman was stubborn and resistant to any sort of help he might offer. Which just made the idea of them going on this trip together a very bad idea.

"I'm sure Louise has other plans," Trey said.

"Plans for what?" Louise straightened and stepped farther into the room.

Before Trey could say anything, Sage launched into an explanation about the trip. Instead of looking put out by the idea, Louise smiled. She liked the idea of dog-sitting?

"I wouldn't mind watching over the little fella," Louise said as though she could read Trey's thoughts. "Would you like that Happy?"

Arf! Arf!

Sage smiled. "Good. Problem solved. Thanks, Louise."

"Yes," Trey said, still trying to accept the inevitable. "Thank you. If I can ever repay the favor just let me know."

There was an ominous twinkle in Louise's eyes when she said, "I will."

He didn't even want to consider what it might mean for him. Something told him that it wouldn't be as simple as picking up coffee or donuts. No, Louise was a sharp lady. When she called in that favor, it would be something meaningful.

"Before I go," Louise said to Sage, "I was wondering if you had the profit and loss statements for the past five years?"

Sage gave Louise a strange look. "Why would you want those? Isn't human resources enough for you? You want to expand into accounting, too?"

"Heavens, no. I ran into Ralph in the hall."

"Ralph, huh?" Sage had a funny tone in her voice and a goofy smile on her face.

Trey had obviously missed something. But it was better that way. The more he got involved in their lives, the harder it'd be when it came time to close the magazine.

"It's not like you think." Louise's voice lacked its normal tone of conviction. "We're friends, is all. I've been married already. And so has he."

"And now you're both widowed. Why not keep each other company?"

Trey chanced a glance at the unusually quiet Louise. For the first time, he witnessed the bold and forthright woman blush. Maybe Sage was on to something.

Avoiding eye contact, Louise said, "Like I'd started to say, Ralph stopped to speak to you and found your door closed. I told him I'd ask you for the documents when I spoke to you."

"Is this for the upcoming audit?"

Louise shrugged. "You're asking the wrong person."

"I wonder why Ralph thinks I'd have those statements," Sage stated, opening and closing desk drawers as though searching for the missing documents. "You'd think those would be kept in the accounting department."

"Mr. Rousseau liked to be in control of everything," Louise supplied. "Have you looked through those file cabinets?" She gestured toward the wall-to-wall line of four-drawer file cabinets.

Trey couldn't help but think that it sounded like his controlling father—always wanting things his way. And when his mother refused, his father didn't care to compromise and just up and left them—left him. The man didn't even give them a backward glance.

Sage turned to Trey. "I hate to give you this task, but could you go through those file cabinets and see if the P&L statements are in there. It's really important that we do well on this audit."

He nodded and set to work. The metal file cabinets were old and the papers inside them were even older. Drawer after drawer, file after file, he searched. And then he opened a drawer that lacked any papers. He was about to close it when a photo caught his attention.

Trey was drawn to the image. It was a photo of himself when he was two or three. He reached for it. The fact that his father had it…should it mean something to him? A spark of hope ignited. In the next breath, he acknowledged that it had been discarded in an old file cabinet. That should be all the answer he needed.

"I see you've found Mr. Rousseau's photos," Sage said from behind him.

Photos? There was more than one? He peered back in the drawer to find his parents' wedding photo and one of him as a baby.

"They were on his desk when I got here. I think he left them because he thought he'd be back once the lawsuit quieted down. I considered messengering them to him, but I didn't want him to read anything into the gesture like I was pushing him out—not after everything he's done for me."

His father had these photos on his desk? But why? Was it for show? That had to be it. No other answer made sense.

"I thought he was estranged from his family?" Trey returned the photo of himself to the drawer. As he did so, he found himself curious about his parents' wedding. Had they been happy at the beginning? He withdrew the framed photo. His father had been smiling like he didn't have a care in the world and Trey's mother…he'd never seen her look happier.

A lump formed in the back of Trey's throat. If they'd been this happy at the start, was he the reason the marriage fell apart?

"I don't know the details." Sage's voice reminded

him that he wasn't alone. "I just know that he talked highly of his son."

Highly? Really? Trey found that so hard to believe. Trey took one last look at the photo. His mother had been so radiant and full of life, nothing like the woman his father had left behind. The broken, lonely woman that Trey had tried to care for.

Trey returned the photo to the drawer. He choked down the rising emotions and closed the drawer, warding off the unhappy memories of his childhood.

"Would you like me to help you search?" Sage offered.

"I've got this." He kept his back to her, not wanting her to read into the expression on his face. "Besides, don't you have a meeting with circulation in ten minutes?"

Sage glanced at the clock. "You're right. I totally forgot."

"No problem. That's what I'm here for."

She grabbed her digital tablet and rushed out of the room.

He was actually grateful for a little time alone. It would give him a chance to shove all those unwanted memories to the back of his mind.

He had no idea why his father had all those photos, but it wasn't because he loved his family. No one that loved their wife and child walked away.

That's why Trey had avoided any sort of committed relationship. He didn't want to be like his father and realize too late that he wasn't cut out to be a family man. No child deserved to be discarded like he'd been.

CHAPTER SIX

ELSA STOOD IN front of her gold-leaf-trimmed mirror. With a finger, she lifted one brow and then she did the same on the other side. Then she drew back her cheeks. It was time for some Botox. She would schedule an appointment for this afternoon.

She picked up her compact and powdered her pointed nose. Perhaps she should do something different with her hair. But then again, why? Could it look any better? It was hard to improve on perfection.

Knock. Knock.

"Come in." It was about time Mr. Hunter arrived for their meeting. He was already ten minutes late. She did not have room in her life for tardiness. Time was money.

The door opened and the hulk of a man stepped inside. "Sorry I'm late. Traffic was snarled."

"I don't care about the traffic. What have you learned about my stepdaughter?"

The man was younger than her. He was tall, dark and in her opinion modestly handsome. Perhaps if she wasn't in such a rush for information, she might enjoy a little alone time with him. But right now she had to deal with her stepdaughter—the girl gave her nothing but a headache.

"Hurry up," Elsa said, anxious to know what Sage had been up to now.

He lifted his digital tablet and consulted his notes. "She's still with *QTR*, but she's on probation. She has to show the board a marked improvement and a solid strategy for the future by the end of the month. And it appears Rousseau's son is taking over the business as CEO."

"A son? I didn't know he had a son. Get me as much information as you can on him." She couldn't have Sage being successful. That wouldn't do. But first she had to gain information and then she'd formulate a plan. "And how did my stepdaughter look?"

"Beautiful." The man's eyes lit up and he smiled as he recalled Sage's image.

Elsa's back teeth ground together. Her gaze narrowed in on the man. "How beautiful?"

"She has grown into the most stunning woman." His voice had a sense of awe in it, which only compounded Elsa's frustration. He rubbed his squared jaw. "She turned heads wherever she went. People seem to fall under her spell whenever she smiles at them."

"She used to do the same thing to her father. She'd smile and he'd do whatever she wanted. He didn't care that as his wife my needs should have come first. It was always all about that brat kid."

"There's something else you should know. Sage is asking questions about you and this company."

The breath caught in Elsa's throat. She knew this day was coming. Once Sage had the means, she would come after Elsa. The girl had to be stopped once and for all.

Elsa turned to the mirror and stared into it. That girl was always trying to ruin everything for her. With an angry groan, Elsa lifted her arm and sent her metal compact crashing into the mirror. Glass shards fell to the floor. If she didn't stop her stepdaughter soon, Sage would have enough clout and money to reveal the truth about how Elsa ascended to CEO of White Publishing. And that could not happen.

Heedless of the mess, Elsa turned to Hunter. Perhaps she should have been paying closer attention to her stepdaughter. She wouldn't make that mistake again. "Do you have someone watching her now?"

"No. You didn't say you wanted twenty-four-hour surveillance—"

"Do I have to spell out everything for you?" she shouted. Her anger and fear bubbled to the surface.

The man's face masked his emotions. "She's leaving for the French Riviera in the morning. Would you like me to follow her?"

Elsa arched a dark brow. "For the Cannes Film Festival?"

Hunter nodded. "From what I gather, she's short-handed and handling the event herself. Well, herself and her male assistant."

Elsa turned her back to the man. Perhaps it was time she had a face-to-face meeting with her stepdaughter. It was time to remind Sage of her proper place in this world—cleaning floors and washing dishes.

"We're both going."

CHAPTER SEVEN

A GENTLE RAIN tap-tapped on the car windows.

Trey leaned back against the seat, wishing the raindrops could wash away the past hurts. He stifled a deep sigh. The truth was that he would rather be anywhere but here. The only consolation was that they'd be staying at a hotel instead of venturing to the château with its abundance of painful memories.

All of Cannes was blanketed in the darkness of night. With the lull of the car engine and the rhythmic tapping of the rain, Trey struggled to keep his eyes open. He'd never learned to sleep on airplanes. And with his seat being separate from Sage's, he'd read a spy novel for most of the flight.

The lights of the city sparkled and glistened in the rain like fine jewels. It was only fitting because his hometown was a treasure on the French Riviera. If only it didn't hold so many painful memories.

He wondered what his mother would think of his plan to bring down the magazine. Would she cheer him on? Or would she be disappointed that he couldn't let go of the past?

Sage pressed a hand to his arm. "Are you okay?"

Trey pushed away the troubling thoughts. "Of course. Why do you ask?"

"Because we've arrived at the hotel and you haven't gotten out of the car."

He glanced out the window at Cannes' finest hotel. When he was a child he imagined this place was a palace and a rich king lived within its walls. Other times, he would pretend his father lived there, taking care of important business, and that one day he'd return home. But in truth, his father never stayed at this hotel that he knew of and his father never came home.

Trey choked down the unwanted rush of emotions. "I think I'm just tired. I can't sleep on planes."

"I guess we have that in common because neither can I."

"Then let's get checked in and we both can get some rest."

He alighted from the car and asked her to get their room keys while he saw to the luggage—all six pieces of it. One piece was his and the rest belonged to Sage. Thankfully some of the suitcases had wheels. How long did she plan to be in France?

Inside, Sage was at the registration counter. From across the lobby, he couldn't hear what was being said, but Sage was talking with her hands and that was never a good sign. Maybe it was a communication problem.

He picked up his speed, hoping to smooth out the situation. He came to a stop next to Sage. "Is there a problem?"

She turned to him with a distinct frown on her face. "I suppose the fact that they gave away our rooms and they have nothing else available could be considered a problem." The frustration in her voice was unmistakable as was the exhaustion written all over her face.

"Let me see what I can do." Perhaps the exchange of French and English had created a miscommunication. He really hoped that was the case. "Did you make the reservation?"

"Yes. But they have no record of it."

"Don't give up just yet."

Sage let out a yawn that spurred Trey into action. But after speaking with both the desk clerk and the manager, they still didn't have any unoccupied rooms for the duration of the festival.

Trey knew with the festival taking place that there wouldn't be any vacancies anywhere in Cannes. There were stories of A-list actors sleeping on the beach because when there's no room available, there's literally nothing available.

Trey had an alternative, but he didn't like it. There was his family's château. He still had a skeleton staff looking after it. He didn't want to keep the place, but he couldn't bring himself to sell it either. It made no sense, but that seemed to be a recurring theme in his life.

He withdrew his phone from his pocket and signaled to Sage that he would be right back. He'd made his housekeeper aware that he was flying in. She was anxious to discuss some issues concerning the château. He told her that he'd stop by when he had a free moment. He'd made it clear he didn't plan to stay at the château so he had no idea what condition the house would be in. On top of that, he didn't know how he'd explain any of this to Sage.

Just take it one problem at a time.

She'd made a mess of things.

Sage mentally kicked herself for not verifying the reservations. She'd meant to, but then she'd gotten distracted.

When Trey returned from making a call, she asked, "Did you come up with alternate lodging?"

"There's nothing available. The city is filled to capacity with festivalgoers."

"Oh." She'd really been hoping his phone call had been productive. "I guess I could do an internet search and start calling them. Maybe I'll get lucky and someone will have a last-minute cancellation."

Trey sighed. "Or you could just come home with me."

"Home? With you?" She sent him a strange look. "I know you're tired, but we're in France not California."

"I know that."

"Then how can I go home with you?"

"Okay, it's not actually my home, but you do recall that I'm from France, right?" He smiled.

Was he inwardly laughing at her? "I didn't forget. The accent gives you away."

"Listen, this banter might be more fun if I wasn't so tired." Before she could dispute the claim, he continued. "My head is pounding, so how about you just agree to come with me?"

It was one thing to stay in the same hotel in separate rooms, but it was much more intimate to share a house. "Are you sure about this?"

"Quite frankly, no. But we can't sleep in the lobby of this hotel."

She hated to admit it but he was right. And she was so tired.

Trey didn't wait for her response as he turned to the door. With the luggage in tow, he headed for an available car. She couldn't help thinking that this was wrong. She knew by the look on his face that taking her with him was the last thing he wanted to do.

There was something growing between them. It was something she didn't want to examine too closely. Though she had a lot of friends, she didn't let anyone get too close. It hurt too much when they betrayed you.

She'd had a boyfriend after she'd finished college. Charlie had been a blond-haired, blue-eyed hunk of a man. At first, she'd resisted him, but every time he'd walked into the coffee shop where she worked in the evenings and on weekends, he flirted with her until he gained her trust. Looking back on that time still hurt.

Charlie had said all the right things—done all the right things, from flowers to fancy dinners. She'd thought at long last she was no longer alone in this world. She'd let down her guard and confided in him about her hopes, dreams and fears.

And then she'd gotten her first official editorial position working for a well-known publisher. It wasn't her beloved White Publishing, but it was a highly sought after position.

She was all set to start in two weeks. And then everything went sideways. Suddenly the company withdrew their job offer with some flimsy excuse about a mix-up.

And then she caught Charlie in a lie followed by a strange text message on his phone. Once confronted by a furious Sage, he confessed to being hired by Elsa to spy on her. And that Elsa was behind the lies that cost her the job. Her stepmother had smeared her name in the publishing world.

There was only one reason her stepmother would still try to hurt her—the woman had a deep dark secret. That day, Sage got all the confirmation she needed that her suspicions about Elsa were true.

She was certain Elsa had lied, cheated and thieved her way to the top of White Publishing. And now Sage would do whatever it cost to out her conniving stepmother—including sacrificing a personal life. That was the day Sage hired her first private investigator.

Once they were in the car headed away from the bright lights, Trey said, "Don't worry. Everything will work out."

She turned to say something, but in the glow of the passing lights she caught his dark, mesmerizing gaze. The words stuck in her throat. Every time he looked into her eyes, she felt as though she were going to drown in his dark brown eyes.

Her pulse quickened and she wondered what it would be like to kiss him. Before now, they'd always been at work where there was a constant string of people in and out of her office. There was no time for indulging in a kiss.

But tonight, all bets were off. She assured herself that exhaustion was playing with her mind. As she continued to stare at him, she knew she wasn't alone with these wayward thoughts.

Though she hadn't dated many men, she did know when they were interested in her. And Trey was interested. Still, there was one more complication—they worked together. And crossing that line would come with a host of complications.

With a sigh, she leaned back against the leather

seat. She just needed some sleep. Tomorrow things would be much clearer.

"We're here." Trey's voice lacked any enthusiasm.

She looked out the window at the impressive château. No expense had been spared in its design or in the landscape that was illuminated with lights lining the drive.

"You said this place belongs to a friend?" She couldn't help wondering what sort of friends Trey had. Obviously they had deep pockets.

"Um…yes." He got out of the car before she could ask any further questions.

As she continued to stare at the château, she wondered about Trey. She craved to know more about him. Who were these friends? Did he have lots of friends? Did he travel overseas often? The questions were endless. Every day there was something new that she wanted to know about him, but she kept stuffing the questions down. It was better if they didn't get to know each other that well—at least, that's what she kept telling herself.

She'd gotten so lost in her thoughts that Trey had time to round the car and open her door for her. She stepped out, glancing around at her new surroundings when a new worry came to her.

"Are you sure your friends won't be upset about you bringing me here without checking with them first?"

He shook his head. "Trust me."

She wanted to trust him. And that surprised her. It'd been a long time since she'd felt that way toward a man.

Trey led the way to the front door. As she followed, a dreadful thought came to mind. Sage swallowed hard and tried to push off the troubling thought. But it wouldn't leave her in peace.

The question that had hovered at the back of her throat refused to be smothered. "Is this your girlfriend's home?"

There was a distinct pause. "I don't have a girlfriend."

It shouldn't have mattered to her, but there was a great sense of relief in his answer. "Your friend must trust you a lot. This place…it's magnificent from the outside. I can't imagine what the inside must be like."

He didn't say anything as he opened the door and stood aside for her to enter. She stared in awe. This place was more than magnificent. It was jaw-dropping, mouth-gaping striking. The foyer was spacious with a gleaming tile floor and stone walls that rose high above her head, forming a dome with a crystal chandelier suspended in the center.

She turned to say something to Trey, but he had stepped back outside to retrieve their luggage from the car. She went out to help.

Trey frowned when he saw her in the rain. "What are you doing out here? You're going to get soaked."

The rain had picked up since they'd arrived just moments ago. But that wasn't enough to deter her. She wasn't used to anyone waiting on her. Since her father died, she'd been the one waiting on people—till she took on the managing editor job at *QTR*. But it was all still so new to her.

It was raining too much to argue. Soon they both had the luggage inside the château. Thankfully she'd packed for all occasions and had a raincoat. She slipped it off and looked around for a place to put it. She couldn't imagine ruining anything in the fancy house that looked more like a museum.

It reminded her of her childhood home in a way. It, too, had been impressive, but her parents had decorated it in a way that was beautiful but comfortable. This château was more a showplace than a home.

She turned to Trey. His face was pale and etched with deep lines that bracketed his eyes and mouth. It was like he'd aged ten years since they'd arrived. What had caused such a reaction?

"Here." Trey held out his hand for her coat. "I'll take it."

He promptly slung it over a chair in the corner. Then he added his coat.

"You can't do that." She rushed over to the chair to retrieve her coat.

"Why not? I'll hang them up tomorrow when they're dry."

"But the chair—"

"Is fine." He sent her a puzzled look. "Why are you so worried about a chair?"

"Because this place—it's like a museum. I don't want to ruin anything and have your friends upset with you." And then she decided to state the obvious. "I can see how worried you are. It's written all over your face."

"There's nothing you can do to this place that will cause a problem. Just relax." He moved to the bottom of the sweeping staircase. "Would you like something to eat? Or should we call it a night?"

The meal on the plane hadn't been much and it had been a while ago, but right now exhaustion was winning. "How about we sleep and then eat?"

"Works for me." He headed up the grand staircase. "There are a lot of bedrooms. You can have your pick as we're the only ones staying here."

"This is an awfully big place just for the two of us."

Maybe staying here wouldn't be so bad. There would be plenty of space and they wouldn't end up on top of each other. And then realizing her wording could be construed in an intimate way, she inwardly groaned. Thankfully she hadn't vocalized her thoughts.

"Is something wrong?" Trey gave her a strange look.

She shook her head. "I'm just tired."

Walking up the flight of steps took considerable effort. She stifled a yawn. She really needed some sleep. She'd be able to think more clearly in the morning. Her head hung low. Right now, she just had to concentrate on putting one foot in front of the other.

At the landing, she bumped right into Trey. Only an inch or two apart, she lifted her head. His brown eyes searched hers. Her heart slammed into her throat, blocking her next breath. If she were to lift up on tiptoes and he were to lower his head, their lips would meet. And at long last, she would know if his kisses were as hot as she imagined.

After all, this was the French Riviera. She couldn't think of a more romantic spot on earth to give in to her fantasy. The pounding of her heart drowned out all of the reasons that this was a bad idea. Maybe Louise was right. Maybe she needed more in her life than work.

And then Trey turned away. He cleared his throat. "There are four rooms to the left and four rooms to your right. Pick whichever one suits you."

"Are you sure? I mean, I don't want to be a bother."

Trey didn't say anything for a moment as though he were lost in his thoughts.

"Trey, what is it?"

He shook his head. "Nothing that can't wait until the morning."

"Are you sure?"

He sent her a smile and nodded.

She started down the wide hallway and stepped in the first bedroom. It was decorated in reds and whites. A large bed sat in the middle of the room with a white comforter and matching pillows. She moved to the bed and sat down. She immediately sunk into the mattress. Wow. Talk about a soft mattress. Not exactly her idea of comfort.

The next room held black and white decor with a red accent. The room was beautiful, but the bed was the exact opposite of the other room. When she sat on the edge, the mattress barely moved.

She caught the amusement in Trey's eyes as she made her way through the rooms.

"Are you just going to follow me around and smile?" She frowned at him.

"I'm just wondering if any of the rooms are going to be up to your standard."

"I'm not normally a picky person."

He nodded, but his eyes said that he didn't believe her.

"I'm not," she insisted as she entered the last bedroom.

She came to a sudden halt. This room was different from the others. There was no striking decor. No fancy pillows or remarkable paintings on the walls. This room, for the lack of a better word, was plain. While one wall was brick like much of the house, the other walls were a smooth plaster in a warm cream color. And the artwork on the walls were photos of different French landscapes.

A large oriental rug stretched out over the hardwood floor and extended under the king-size bed. The bed faced a set of French doors that were slightly ajar, letting in the fresh sea air. And overhead were exposed beams running the length of the ceiling. She never would have put this room in the same group as the others as its atmosphere was so different—so relaxed.

But the telling sign was in the mattress. She walked over to the bed and sat down. It wasn't too soft or too hard. It was perfect.

She smiled. "This is it."

Trey's brow arched. "Are you sure? This room isn't as nice as the other ones."

"That's one of the things I like about it. And the bed is perfect." Then realizing that he might have been planning to stay here, she said, "Unless you were planning to sleep here."

"No." He said it rather quickly. "I'll just grab your things."

"I can get them."

He shook his head. "Tonight you're my guest."

She was so tired that she didn't have the energy to argue with him. If he was that anxious to carry all her suitcases upstairs, more power to him.

In the meantime, she'd just lean back on the bed

and rest for a moment. It had been such a long, long day or was it two days now? She wasn't sure with the long layovers and the time change.

Maybe she'd just close her eyes for a moment…

Of all the bedrooms, why did she have to pick that one?

Trey frowned as he struggled to get all five of her suitcases up the stairs. The woman really needed to learn how to pack lighter. He didn't think he owned enough clothes to fill five suitcases. Okay, so maybe they were planning to be here for two weeks, but there was such a thing as a laundry machine.

At the top of the steps, he paused. It was a good thing he exercised daily. He rolled the cases back along the hallway to the very familiar bedroom. The door was still ajar.

"Sage, it's just me." He would have knocked but his hands were full trying to keep a hold on all the luggage.

There was no response. Maybe she'd decided to explore the rest of the house. Or perhaps she was standing out on the balcony. It was one of his favorite spots to clear his head.

But two steps into the room, he stopped.

There was Sage stretched across his bed. Her long dark hair was splayed across the comforter. He knew he shouldn't stare, but he couldn't help himself. She was so beautiful. And the look on her face as she was sleeping was one of utter peace. It was a look he'd never noticed during her wakeful hours. If you knew her, you could see something was always weighing on her mind. And he'd hazard a guess that it went much deeper than the trouble with the magazine.

Though he hated to admit it, he was impressed with the new format that she'd rolled out for the magazine. Instead of it being a trashy rag, it now had integrity and, at times, it was a platform to promote social change for the positive.

But he wasn't ready to back down on his campaign to close the magazine's doors. None of it changed the fact that to hurt his father in the same manner that he'd hurt him, the magazine had to go. It had been Trey's objective for so many years. He never thought he'd be in a position to make it happen—but now as the new CEO of QTR International, he was in the perfect position to make his father understand in some small way the pain his absence had inflicted on him.

Trey's thoughts returned to the gorgeous woman lying on his bed sound asleep. She was the innocent party—the bystander who would get hurt—and he had no idea how to protect her. The only thing he did know was that the longer he kept up this pretense of being her assistant instead of the heir to the QTR empire—the worse it was going to be when the truth finally won out—and it would.

The truth always came to light—sometimes at the most inopportune times.

The burden of his secret weighed heavy on his shoulders. He moved quietly in the room, placing the luggage in the corner. And then he turned back to Sage. It'd been a long time since he'd had a woman in his bed. And this time he wouldn't even have the pleasure of joining her.

Although, there was no way she could sleep in that position with her feet dangling off the edge of the bed with her high heels still on. Should he wake her? He glanced at her face. She looked so contented.

He moved quietly across the floor. He knelt down next to her. His hand wrapped around her calf, enjoying the smoothness of her skin. And then realizing he was letting himself get distracted, he slipped off one shoe. She never missed a slow, steady breath. He then repeated the same process with the other leg.

Somehow he had to get her legs on the bed without waking her. Apparently she was more wiped out than he'd imagined. As he settled her comfortably on the bed, all she did was roll away from him. Her summer dress rode high up on her creamy thigh and suddenly his mouth went dry.

Turn away. Forget it. She's off-limits.

His mind said all the right things, but the rest of him was tempted to wake her—to see if she was as attracted to him as he was to her. The devil and angel played advocates in his mind. After all, she didn't know who he really was. But it wouldn't be right to start things under a false premise, no matter how casual it might be.

He draped the soft fabric of the bedspread over her. And then he noticed that a few strands of hair had strayed across her face. He should just leave her be, but his fingers tingled with temptation. He reached out and ever so gently swept the hair back. And then he turned and headed for the door.

CHAPTER EIGHT

Sage awoke slowly.

She was warm but not too warm. And the bed was soft but not too soft.

And best of all, she was wrapped in very strong, capable arms. She opened her eyes and gazed into coffee-brown eyes. Her heart fluttered in her chest. She didn't know that she could be this happy.

Trey smiled at her as his fingers stroked her cheek. His thumb traced over her bottom lip, sending a bolt of desire through her core. The truth was that she'd never get enough of him. Trey was everything she'd ever dreamed about—and more.

Her hand reached out to him. Her palm pressed against his bare chest. She could feel his heart. It was still pounding with need. Her fingers inched up his muscled chest until her hand wrapped around his neck, pulling him closer to her.

As she scooted closer to him to press her lips to his, he disappeared. Her hand landed on the empty spot in the bed. Where had he gone? Her gaze searched the room but it was empty. Once again she was all alone.

"Trey! Trey!"

The next thing she knew she was being jostled. "Sage, wake up. It's a dream."

Her eyes blinked open. "Trey?"

"Yeah. It's me." He sent her a reassuring smile. "It was just a nightmare. Do you remember what it was about?"

She remembered every delicious detail and it was certainly no nightmare. And she also remembered that, in the end, he'd left her. Just like the other people in her life.

She shook her head. "It's a blur." She glanced down, finding herself still dressed in the clothes from yesterday. "It looks like I fell asleep on you last night." And then she realized how that sounded as heat rushed to her cheeks. "I, uh, must have been more tired than I thought."

"No problem."

Her gaze moved to the man who starred in her very hot dream. Her face grew warmer. Why did Trey have to be the man of her dreams? Now how was she supposed to act professional around him knowing she secretly desired him?

Don't make a big deal of it. He can't read your thoughts. Just act normal.

She took in his smart-looking suit. "It looks like you're all ready to face the day."

"I've been up for a while." A serious expression came over his face. "Sage, we need to talk."

Oh, no. What exactly had she said in her sleep? She didn't want to know. Nope. Not at all.

She scrambled to climb out of the other side of

the bed. "Sorry I'm running late. Just let me grab a quick shower and I'll be ready to go."

"You don't have to rush—"

"Sure, I do." She moved to her suitcases, which were waiting for her in the corner of the room. "We have to get our badges."

"We have all day."

"It can be a long wait since they have to take our photo. Besides, this is a good day to catch some people before they get caught up in the movie premieres and the parties."

He arched a brow. "How would you know?"

She shrugged. "I attended the festival with my father. It was a long time ago, but I still remember parts of it. And one of those memories was waiting in line at the Accreditation Centre. I take it you've never attended?"

He hesitated. "I've attended the festival."

"Then you should know we have a lot to do today."

"If you say so." Trey moved to the door. "I'll get us some breakfast."

"Just coffee for me."

"You need more than that since we'll be walking to the festival." When she sent him a surprised look, he added, "A lot of the roads will be closed. Walking will be our fastest option."

"Okay. I'll be down in a few minutes." If she could just get them away from this very cozy setting and into the public, things would smooth out. And hopefully Trey would forget about her calling out his name and whatever else she'd said in her sleep.

"We'll see about that."

Before she could say another word, the door snicked shut. Alone again. She sighed. She looked at all of her luggage. Perhaps she had brought a lot of clothes but she knew she had to dress smartly. So her roommates had loaned her a few dresses, creating an extensive, all-event wardrobe.

Her and her two roommates routinely shared clothes. On a tight budget, it made clothes go a lot further. But if she could keep *QTR* on its upward swing, her finances wouldn't be quite so strained. Of course, her latest private investigator looking into her stepmother was taking a large bite out of each paycheck. She'd instructed him to look under every rock until he found what Elsa was hiding.

Sage placed a suitcase on the large bed and opened it. With her arm full of dresses, she moved to the wall of closets and found half of them filled with men's clothes. It must be the owner's. Thankfully there was enough room for her things.

Not wanting to keep Trey waiting much longer, she didn't bother with the other suitcases. They could be dealt with later.

* * *

He never expected to hear Sage calling out his name in her sleep.

Trey had no idea what to make of it.

Her tone hadn't been one of passion. Instead there had been an urgency to her voice. So if she was having a nightmare, why would she cry out to him? It was just one more thing for him to ponder about his beautiful boss.

They had just collected their photo badges and were standing outside the doors of the Cannes Exhibition Centre. Sage was pleased to find their badges were marked with a red dot containing the letter *R*. It granted them access to red-carpet screenings.

Trey may have grown up in Cannes, but he'd never been that involved with the festival. So, much like Sage, he was figuring it out as they went along.

People strolled by in stylish clothes. Some were famous, others weren't. All smiled brightly when there was a camera pointed in their direction.

He glanced over at Sage as a smile lit up her face. She wasn't wasting any time trying to save her… er…*his* magazine. He didn't like that they were on opposite sides of keeping the magazine. Still, he couldn't help but applaud her resilience.

"Hello." Sage stepped forward and held out her hand to the female lead in an upcoming action film. "I'm Sage White with *QTR Magazine*—"

The young actress immediately withdrew her hand. "I can't talk to you. I've heard about your magazine."

"But you don't understand—"

"I understand enough." The young woman turned and walked away as fast as she could on those five-inch heels.

Sage turned a worried gaze in his direction. He didn't know what to tell her. His father had done quite a number on the magazine—taking it from stellar reporting to the depths of heresy. They were lucky his father hadn't put headlines of UFO sightings on the cover.

The magazine had been in Trey's family for generations. Each generation had made their mark on it. Way, way back in the beginning, the magazine had started here in France.

A few generations later, it had been relocated to the States. New York to be exact. But then Trey's great-grandfather had moved it to Los Angeles. He was a big fan of John Wayne. But when it came time for Trey's father to put his mark upon the publication, it was all about profits. It didn't matter how he got them. He'd taken the Rousseau name and dragged it through the mud.

And now it was up to Trey to put an end to it all. But perhaps Sage's idea for the magazine wasn't a bad one—but would anyone even give her a chance?

As time went by, she didn't get past a greeting before people moved on.

"Perhaps we should try again tomorrow," Trey said, feeling bad for her. "When people aren't in such a rush."

"I can't stop now. I haven't even gained one new contact."

He'd give her a gold star for effort. "But it's only the first day of the festival. People are still getting settled in. There are still ten more days to go."

"I know. But I had a goal to gain at least one good contact per day. You don't understand how important this is." Sage started walking.

Trey kept pace with her. "Maybe you're putting too much pressure on yourself."

She cast him a sideways glance. "You don't believe that, do you?"

He did believe it, but he also knew she wasn't in the mood to hear his observations right now.

He reached in his jacket pocket and pulled out a small envelope. "Perhaps this will help."

She had to admit that she was very curious. "What is it?"

"I've secured us an invitation to the Red Heart Gala tonight."

"You what?" Her mouth gaped. "But that party is totally exclusive. I heard some of the stars couldn't even get invitations."

"See. The problem with them is they don't know the right people." He sent her a big smile.

"And who might that be?"

"I don't know if you can be trusted with this highly sensitive information. If it leaks out, I might lose my source." He winked, letting her know that he was teasing her.

"I swear no one will hear from me. Now spill."

"It's Maria."

"Maria?" It took her a second to figure out who he meant. "You mean, Maria—that works at the château?"

He laughed. "Yes. The one and the same."

"But I don't understand."

"Maria is a part of the housekeeper network. If you need something, her group can definitely pull it off. They are amazing and highly resourceful."

"I'm totally impressed. These tickets are highly sought after. Anyone who is anyone will be there."

"And that's why we'll be there."

"You mean to try and gain some interviews?"

He shook his head. "Not tonight. It will be all about enjoying yourself and just soaking up some of the atmosphere. No stressing. No worrying. And no working."

"But—"

He held up a hand, stopping her protest. "There are no *buts*. Those are the rules or we don't go."

"I still have one *but*."

He didn't want more problems. "What is it?"

"But I don't have a red dress to wear. I have black, blue, turquoise and deep purple but no red." When he sent her a puzzled look, she said, "The dress code is red, except for the men. Black tux is mandatory. You do have at least one tux with you, don't you?"

He nodded. "I made sure of it before we left LA."

"So that just leaves me with nothing to wear."

Trey told her about a couple of local dress shops. They agreed to meet up later at the château. As soon as she walked away, he reached for his phone to call ahead and tell them to charge him for anything Sage picked out. But then he paused. How would he explain that to Sage since he hadn't found the right time to tell her about his true identity? He slipped his phone back in his pocket.

The evening was amazing.

Sage and Trey had walked the red carpet and posed for a photo. Trey explained that even though they weren't famous, the photographers made money selling the photos back to the people. Sage had to admit that she would be buying the photo— most definitely. She never wanted to forget this amazing experience.

She never imagined she'd be in the same room with so many stars. It was dizzying trying to name all the celebrities. And the fact that she was speaking with them as though she were one of them—well, it was a night she'd never forget.

The hotel where the gala was being held was the same one where she was supposed to be staying. The architecture was stunning. Marble pillars supported an intricately designed ceiling. And one crystal chandelier wouldn't do for this ballroom. Instead, there were at least a dozen. This place was fit for royalty.

She glanced down at her deep-red full-length gown, wondering if she was dressed appropriately.

Her visit to the boutique let her know that she couldn't afford anything in the store, even if she had maxed out her credit card. But the salesgirl, having noticed the distress written on Sage's face, told her about a little out-of-the-way shop where secondhand dresses were sold for a fraction of the original price.

It was where Sage had found this off-the-shoulder, figure-hugging gown with a daring slit up her left thigh. It didn't fit exactly, but a few strategically placed pins in the bodice held it in place. And luckily, she had a pair of black stilettos that paired perfectly with the dress. She actually felt like Cinderella at the ball. Did that make him her prince?

Her heart fluttered in her chest. The most handsome man of all was the one holding her in his very capable arms. She lifted her head and stared up at Trey as he guided them around the dance floor.

"Are you enjoying yourself?" Trey's voice broke through her thoughts.

"I am. I don't think my feet have touched the ground since we arrived." She leaned in closer. "Did you see the jewels people are wearing?"

Trey smiled and nodded as they practically floated past the white marble columns surrounding the dance floor.

"Look at that." She pointed at the enormous chandelier made up of thousands of crystals. "I love how the light dances off it. Now that is flashy."

A smile lifted his lips and smoothed the lines on his face.

"What are you smiling about?"

"You. I've never seen you so…" He hesitated as though searching for the right word.

"Awestruck? Impressed?" Then she moved her hand, stroking her fingers down over his soft beard. "Captivated?"

His dark eyes lit up as though her touch awakened a part of him. His gaze dipped to her lips. Her pulse quickened. She had a feeling this night was just getting started.

She couldn't turn away. My, he was handsome. So handsome and sweet that her reservations about trusting him slipped from her mind. Tonight, they were no longer boss and assistant. Tonight, he was just Trey—a devastatingly handsome escort with a twinkle in his eyes. And she was just Sage, his date.

So was there any reason not to let down her guard and treat him as she would any man who caught her eye and dazzled her with the most amazing night?

The lyrics from the next song wrapped around them. Their bodies swayed gently to the tune. As her body brushed against the hard plains of Trey, the breath caught in her throat. Every nerve ending in her body was stimulated.

In that moment, with his hand pressed lightly to the bare skin at the small of her back, she couldn't think of any reason not to give in to her desire. She stopped dancing. She lifted her chin and their gazes caught.

Questions reflected in his dark eyes. His mouth opened to say something, but nothing came out. The next thing she knew his head was lowering toward hers and she was lifting up on her tiptoes. When their lips met, it was like a powerful jolt of electricity zapped through her body.

She had never felt this way with any other man. Trey was unique in so many ways. And she never wanted this magical night to end.

His lips moved slowly over hers. His touch was soft and teasing. A need grew within her. She wanted more of him. All of him—

The band stopped. A round of applause filled the room, jolting both Sage and Trey back to reality. With great reluctance, Sage pulled back.

Her lips tingled as Trey led her from the now-empty dance floor. She had no idea where they went from here, but she was anxious to find out.

They spent the rest of the evening mingling, dancing and sipping bubbly while eating the most delicious hors d'oeuvres, but sadly there was to be no more kissing.

Sage was surprised at her eagerness to taste him once more and was disappointed that Trey didn't feel the same. Because as soon as they arrived at the château, Trey mumbled something about needing to send an email and he disappeared, leaving her alone with her thoughts.

She'd messed up. She knew it. Crossing that line between them was a mistake. Going forward, she was going to have to do better.

CHAPTER NINE

THE NEXT MORNING Trey knew he had to say something to Sage about the kiss. He'd seen the confused look in her eyes when he'd backed off and when he'd made a quick exit after they'd arrived home.

It wasn't that he didn't want to follow that kiss up with more—a lot more. The problem was that Sage didn't know the "real" man she was about to get involved with. And if they were about to start something, even casually as he didn't do commitments, then she deserved all the facts.

After watching his parents, he didn't believe in living happily-ever-after. Love was fleeting at best—at worst it crushed people. Either way, he refused to end up on the losing end like his mother.

And this morning, Sage was acting differently—cooler. They had just finished breakfast and headed for the festival when he decided to lay everything on the line.

"Sage, we need to talk."

"I know. We were so busy with the festival yesterday that I didn't get to touch base with you about the audit prep work. Is it all coming together?"

"Yes. But this isn't about the audit—"

"Good. I'll check my emails when we head back

to the château to dress for this evening's movie premiere."

"Sage, wait." And then realizing how abrupt that sounded, he said, "Please. What I want to talk about isn't work—"

"Stop." She quit talking and turned to him. "I know that I crossed a line. It was wrong of me. It won't happen again."

"Sage, if you'd let me speak."

"No. Just let it go. Please. It was just a lapse of judgment. It didn't mean anything." When he didn't say anything, she continued. "I just got caught up in the excitement of the evening."

So he'd misread the situation? Good. They could get back on track.

"So how about we get to work," he said, wanting to end this awkward conversation.

"We're okay?" Her gaze searched his.

He nodded. "Let's go."

They continued toward the festival. Trey shoved aside the awkward moment with Sage. It was best not to dwell on it. But still, a strained silence lingered between them.

When they reached the Grand Theatre Lumière for the morning showing, Trey excused himself to get them both coffee. The truth was that he needed a few moments alone to gather his thoughts.

Meanwhile, Sage had zeroed in on a young actress and planned to go introduce herself. He hoped it went well. Wait. There he went again, wishing for Sage to succeed. Was that really what he wanted?

The line at the café was long. Fifteen minutes later, Trey stepped up to the counter. He ordered espresso for himself and a vanilla latte for Sage.

He was on his way back when he spotted a tall, slender woman approaching Sage. The woman had her back to him, but she was much taller than Sage. In fact, the woman was almost as tall as him. Her willowy figure was draped in a snug black dress. Her platinum-blond hair was cut short and not a strand was out of place.

He paused near one of the large pillars outside the theater. If this woman happened to be an actress or person of interest, he didn't want to interrupt Sage's chance to nail down an interview.

He could only hope this was the break Sage had been hoping for. It would be a good way to ease the tension between them. And then they could go home and what? He'd reveal the truth of his identity to her?

How exactly would that go?

She'd most likely fire him. And that would be the easy part. The other part—the one where there is pain and possible tears in her eyes—well, he wasn't so sure that he was up for that.

He moved a little closer. Neither of the women appeared to notice him.

"Sage, my dear, what are you doing here?" The

older woman's voice held an icy tone. "Shouldn't you be off cleaning floors or some such thing?"

This woman knew Sage? And then the woman turned, giving Trey a full view of her face. It was Elsa White.

His body tensed. He wanted to move to Sage's defense. But at that moment, Sage's gaze met his and she gave a slight shake of her head, warning him off.

Standing on the sidelines was not a position he was used to taking. When it came to caring for his mother, he may have been young but he'd stepped up, making sure she made her doctors' appointments and took her medicine. But Sage wasn't like his mother. Sage was strong and more than capable of taking care of herself.

Sage's face instantly hardened. There was absolutely no sign of that famous smile that she shared with everyone. "Elsa, I didn't expect to see you here."

Trey couldn't have been dragged from his spot. If Sage needed him, he'd step up. But he wasn't the only one to notice the exchange. These two women were oblivious to the observers. Right now, their sole focus was on each other.

His gaze volleyed between them. There was so much tension arcing between these women that it could light up all of Cannes. To say there was no love lost between these two was an understatement.

"You shouldn't be here," Elsa said. "You don't belong."

"I'm right where I need to be. Shouldn't you be in New York plotting your next devious deal?"

Anger lit up Elsa's eyes before they narrowed with an evil glint. "I don't have to be in New York to do my plotting. You are out of your league here. You best be on your way little girl."

Sage squared her shoulders and lifted her chin. "I'm not a child anymore. Your scare tactics no longer work on me."

"Oh, dear, you misunderstand me. I'm not trying to scare you. I'm warning you to get out of my way before I roll right over you."

And with that the older woman turned and strode away.

Sage stood there for a moment as though gathering her thoughts. Trey approached her. He really wanted to question her, but he knew now wasn't the right moment. She would open up to him when she was ready and not a moment sooner.

Sage began to walk and he fell in step beside her. She was quiet for a moment. She didn't stop until they were at an overlook. The morning sun danced upon the water. The multitude of yachts looked like toy boats from this distance. But Trey's attention was on Sage and what he could do for her.

She paused at the railing. "I'm sorry about that. I seem to be making a habit of apologizing to you."

He handed her the latte. "Don't be sorry. You didn't do anything wrong."

"I'm sure you're wondering about that woman back there." Sage continued to stare straight ahead, not giving him a chance to look into her eyes.

"It's okay. You don't have to talk about it." He meant it. Even though he was curious, he had never seen Sage so upset. It was best to let the subject rest.

"You're right. I don't want to talk about her." Sage glanced at him. Determination reflected in her gaze. "But I have to."

"Okay. I'm listening."

She took a sip of her coffee. "Elsa is my stepmother. My mother died when I was young. And for many years, my father and I were alone. Then one day my father tells me that he met someone. I was genuinely happy for him. I knew how lonely he was without my mother."

"It couldn't have been easy for either of you."

"His relationship with Elsa could only be described as a whirlwind romance. At first, Elsa was friendly. It wasn't until much later that I realized it was all a show—at least where I was concerned. I never figured out if she cared about my father or if he only constituted a ticket to a better life. I hope she truly loved him because he must have loved her."

"Why do you say that?"

"Because growing up, he used to take me to the office of White Publishing and he'd tell me that one day it would be all mine. He said it was my legacy. And then when he unexpectedly died of a heart attack, the will was read and the company and house…" She paused as though to rein in her emotions. "It all went to Elsa. I was gutted. I… I felt so betrayed."

"How old were you?"

"I was sixteen. I went from private schools to public. I lost all my friends. And when I wasn't in school, I was cleaning the house. Elsa got rid of the staff, saying that we had to tighten the purse strings as the business was in trouble." Sage turned to him with sadness reflected in her eyes. "You don't want to hear all of this."

"I do, if you want me to."

"For my eighteenth birthday, Elsa kicked me out. At the time, my shares of White Publishing were worth pennies per share. Not having a cent to my name, I was forced to sell her my shares in order to eat. To this day, I regret that decision. When I signed those shares over, I handed over any right to my legacy. But at the time, I was so young and scared. I didn't know how to take care of myself. I learned really fast."

"I wish I had known you then."

"Why?" She eyed him suspiciously. "Would you have ridden up on your white horse to save me?"

He shrugged. "I don't ride horses, but maybe a white car."

She didn't laugh at his attempt to lighten the mood. "I didn't need someone to save me. I needed to save myself. I needed to learn that even without my father's money, I would be all right. I learned a lot about myself in those years."

"But you shouldn't have had to."

Sage turned to face the sea. "Maybe I did. I'll be the first to admit that my father spoiled me. I had no idea how much so until I had to feed myself and put a roof over my head. In that manner, Elsa did me a favor."

"Don't go giving that woman any compliments. She's pure evil."

"Maybe. But I learned that I'm stronger than I ever thought. I worked for a maid service throughout college. With a full-time job, it took me five years to earn my degree, including taking summer classes. It wasn't easy, but I did it. Now, I won't give up until I have White Publishing back."

He had a feeling that his smiling, beautiful boss was plotting something and it worried him. He'd heard Elsa was not a person to be crossed. "Sage, what are you up to?"

She shook her head. "It's nothing for you to worry about. Everything is going according to plan. By the way, I just landed an exclusive interview with Starr. Isn't that great?"

"Yes, but don't underestimate Elsa."

Sage's eyes widened. "How do you know about my stepmother?"

"Everyone has heard the rumors of Elsa White. She's notorious in the business and not in a good way." He stared deep into Sage's eyes, imploring her to heed his warning. He'd dealt with his own share of powerful enemies. "Just keep your eyes open."

"Trey?" a male voice called out behind him. "Trey? Is that you?"

With the greatest regret, he pulled back from Sage. He knew by coming to the festival that he would likely run into someone he knew. But with his quiet social calendar, he didn't think there would be many people that would recognize him.

He mouthed, *I'm sorry*, to Sage.

Her normally bright eyes dimmed. "I… I need to get back to the festival and circulate." She glanced over his shoulder at the person approaching. "Don't rush on my account."

He turned to find his childhood friend. They'd been roommates one year at boarding school, but then Sam had moved away. Trey had always wondered what had happened to him.

"I thought that was you." Sam strode up to him all smiles, just as Trey remembered him.

"It's good to see you."

They started with a handshake that ended up in a hug and a clap on the back.

Trey pulled back. His gaze quickly scanned the crowd, searching for Sage, but she was nowhere to be found. He really needed to straighten things out with her.

"So what has you here?" Sam asked.

"Work."

Sam glanced at his press badge. "You decided to work for your father?"

It had been no secret in school that no love was lost between him and his father. When family days rolled around, he was the only one who had no family show up. His father was too involved with his precious magazine and his mother never felt up to traveling. As far back as he could remember, his mother never felt well.

"Something like that." Anxious to turn the conversation away from himself, Trey said, "How about you?"

"I'm producing films."

Trey thought back in time. "You always did have a flair for acting."

"Yeah. But it appears that I'm better behind the scenes."

Trey thought of how he'd turned into an actor with Sage. It had all seemed innocent enough in the beginning. But now that he'd gotten to know her—to kiss her—it all felt wrong.

When he confessed that he was out to destroy the magazine she'd been working so hard to rebuild, she would hate him. But was he at a point where he could just let go of the revenge that he'd been plotting against his father since he was in boarding school?

CHAPTER TEN

THE DEEPEST, DARKEST night had settled upon Cannes.

Elsa stood on the balcony of her deluxe suite enjoying the inky blackness. She lifted her second glass of cognac to her lips and took a healthy sip. The heady liquid hit the back of her throat and burned as it went down. She smiled.

So far her time in Cannes had been utterly boring—well, there was that run-in with Sage. That had been slightly amusing. It would have been more fun if the girl had grown a backbone.

Elsa recalled how Sage had always thought the world was made of rainbows and butterflies. Elsa expelled a frustrated sigh. Whoever thought a kind word or smile could open doors? Only Sage. That foolish, foolish girl.

Knock. Knock.

She moved to the door. Her long, silk robe fluttered around her legs as she crossed the room. Elsa yanked the door open to find Mr. Hunter standing there in a dark suit. The top buttons of his shirt were undone, giving her a glimpse of his chest. Not bad. Not bad at all. His hair had been cut and styled. He really was rather handsome.

Why hadn't she noticed this before? Perhaps the alcohol was skewing her perception or maybe she'd never been so bored and anxious for something to amuse her. Yes, Mr. Hunter just might serve a dual purpose this evening.

But first, they had to get business out of the way.

"What have you learned about my stepdaughter? Has she heeded my warning? Is she leaving?"

"No. She's still here. And I have learned something very interesting."

The way he said the words sparked Elsa's interest. "Is it something I can use against her?"

"I think it is."

Elsa smiled. This man was getting more attractive by the moment. "Come here and sit with me on the couch." She sat down and patted a spot next to her. Once he was seated, she leaned in close to him and inhaled his spicy aftershave. Mmm… He smelled divine. Tonight was definitely looking up. She traced a manicured nail over the slight stubble on his cheek, down his neck and then played with the few hairs on his chest—his very firm chest. "What delicious information have you uncovered?"

Hunter cleared his throat. "Well, it appears her assistant isn't actually her assistant after all. But I don't think she knows it. In fact, I'm certain she doesn't."

Elsa undid a button on his shirt. "If you make this good, I promise you'll receive a bonus you'll never forget."

Hunter's dark eyes met hers. There was the fire of desire burning in them, which only excited Elsa more. She loved when she could control people, whether it was in the office or in bed.

She leaned forward, pressing her lips to his. There was no gentle foreplay. There was hunger. Need. And lust. And he was going to do just fine for scratching her itch.

She pulled back. "Now explain your cryptic remark. Her assistant isn't really her assistant. How is that possible?"

"For some reason that I don't understand, the man acting as Sage's assistant is really Quentin Thomas Rousseau III."

Elsa leaned back on the couch. Her mind was racing a mile a minute. "And you say Sage doesn't know his true identity?"

Hunter shook his head. "Not as far as I can tell."

"Very interesting." So what was the young Rousseau up to? Was he going to be an asset to her plans? Or had he fallen under Sage's spell like so many men before him?

"I need all the information you can find about the young Rousseau. Is there anything else I should know about?"

"Actually, Sage just landed a most sought after interview with Starr."

This news darkened Elsa's mood. She got to her feet and moved to the drink cart to refill her cognac. She took a mouthful of the fiery liquid and swallowed. Her gaze lifted to the mirror that hung over the drink cart. Elsa stared at her beautiful image. Usually it made her feel better, but not tonight. As she smoothed an errant strand of hair behind her ear, she couldn't help but think of her stepdaughter. Maybe the girl had grown more of a backbone than she'd originally thought.

"This interview, will it help her magazine?"

Hunter nodded. "Definitely. From what I gather, it should be a cover spot."

Still holding the glass of cognac, Elsa's hand tightened around the crystal glass. How dare that worthless girl try and beat her in her own arena. Elsa was the queen of publishing. There was no room for Sage.

Elsa caught her image in the mirror. For a moment, she looked older—second best. Anger pumped through her veins.

Elsa turned to Hunter. "I want you to set up an appointment with the actress before her interview with Sage. I don't care what she has planned. Tell her to cancel it."

Hunter's dark eyes widened as though to complain about not being her secretary. But as though he sensed the danger in disagreeing with her at that moment, he said, "I will go take care of it now."

"Not yet." She strode toward him in her stilettos. "I have something else in mind for you."

She had to do something with all of her pent-up energy or she would explode. When she reached him, she placed a hand behind his head and pulled him down to her lips.

And tomorrow—tomorrow I will deal with Sage. She will not win. Never!

CHAPTER ELEVEN

THREE DAYS OF being brushed off by celebrities.

But today would be different.

Sage had the feeling everything was about to change and she chose to believe it was going to be in a good way. She might not have gotten much sleep after attending a party until the wee hours of the morning, but she felt as though she could conquer the world.

And then there was Trey. Try as she might to forget the kiss and his reaction, it was there with her every day, lurking in the shadows of her mind. But there had been no mention of it and things were getting back to normal.

It was best that she centered her thoughts on work. It always brought her comfort. Tomorrow was her big interview with Starr. She'd already arranged to have the photographer meet them. And just so she didn't miss anything in her notes, she was going to have Trey record the session. It was all going to work out and this interview was just the beginning. Today she hoped to secure another interview. It was the only way to keep the magazine alive.

She was due for some good luck. Taking a positive attitude, she was singing a tune as she came down the stairs at the château. Not finding Trey inside, she made her way to the veranda. Trey was sitting there reading something on his phone while drinking a cup of coffee.

As soon as he saw her, he put his phone down. "Did I just hear you sing 'Heigh-Ho'?"

She couldn't help but smile. "You must be hearing things."

He sent a disbelieving look. "I know what I heard."

Trying to change the subject, she asked, "Are you ready to set off to work?"

He gave her another funny look. "I am."

She couldn't help but notice how dashing he looked in a pair of dark slacks and a white dress shirt with the top buttons undone and the sleeves rolled up. It was then that she noticed his watch. It was a designer watch. She'd noticed it before and assumed that it was a knockoff. A very good knockoff.

Trey got to his feet and rounded the table to pull a chair out for her. "But you're not. I'll just have Maria bring out your breakfast."

She was about to protest, but then reconsidered. Perhaps a bite to eat before the interview would be helpful. "Thanks."

"No problem."

In just a couple of minutes, he returned with an apple in his hand.

"Is that all you're eating?" She hated the thought of Maria going out of her way to cook for just her.

"Relax. I already ate."

"Oh." She eyed up the bright red apple. "You must really like apples. You seem to always have one on hand."

"They're a sweet snack and travel easy. You should try them."

"I eat apples."

He arched a disbelieving brow.

"Okay, not very often. Since when have you come to know my habits so well?"

"Since we've been working practically nonstop to get the magazine turned around."

Just then Maria came onto the veranda with a covered dish and a large glass of fresh squeezed orange juice. As Sage ate the delicious food, she realized that staying here at the château reminded her a lot of her childhood. There had been glamorous travels to the farthest ends of the earth and her spacious childhood home had been complete with a full staff that were more like family than hired help. But most of all, she'd been able to relax and enjoy herself.

"What are you thinking about?" Trey asked once Maria departed.

Why not be honest with him? No matter what she wanted to tell herself, they were much more than coworkers. Friends? Possibly. But somehow it felt like more. She knew that reading anything into their relationship was dangerous. For all she knew Elsa could have planted Trey in her life. It wouldn't be the first time that her stepmother had done such a despicable thing. But there was something about Trey—a genuineness that made her want to trust him with her deepest and most profound secrets.

She set aside her fork. "I was thinking that I haven't been this relaxed since…since before my father married Elsa."

Trey didn't say anything. Instead he settled back in his chair as though letting her open up to him at her own pace.

She averted her gaze out to the sea. "After my father's marriage to Elsa, the changes to the household didn't happen all at once. In fact, in the beginning Elsa couldn't have been nicer and Father had been so happy. All those years of loneliness were behind him. But when my father traveled for business, Elsa started to change. Things in my room started to disappear."

"She stole from you?" Trey's expression was one of astonishment.

"When I called her out on it, she was all apologetic. She claimed there was a charity drive and she didn't think I would mind donating a few items to the underprivileged. Of course, looking back now I realize this was all for my father's benefit. She was so cunning and devious that, in the end, she had me feeling guilty for wanting my possessions back—including the last gift from my mother—a porcelain doll."

Trey's expression hardened. "Is it all right if I hate your stepmother on your behalf?"

Sage shrugged. "I struggle with that emotion every time the woman interferes in my life, which was quite often over the years. But to hate her would consume me and hurt me, not her. Instead I feel bad for her that she is such a miserable, spiteful person."

Trey's mouth gaped slightly. "You feel sorry for her?"

Sage nodded. "Not like I want to help her or anything. I still think she has a lot to answer for, but sorry as in I'm grateful I can see the good in life, unlike her, and I'm not consumed with revenge or whatever drives her."

Trey leaned forward, resting his elbows on the table. He reached out and placed his hand on hers. His thumb gently stroked the back of her hand, sending goose bumps racing up her arms and setting her heart aflutter.

His voice was low and gravelly when he said, "Have I ever told you how amazing I find you?"

Right now, with him touching her, she was having problems stringing words together. "Me?"

"Yes, you. It seems like no matter what life

throws at you, you find a way to keep going—to keep smiling."

Just then she smiled. She didn't mean to. It just happened. And then her gaze caught his and her heart vaulted into the back of her throat. If there hadn't been a table between them, she was certain she would have thrown herself into his arms.

And how would Trey react? Would he push her away? Or would he draw her close. With his hand on hers, her signals were getting confused.

"Sage, there's something we need to talk about."

"Is it about the interview?"

"No. It's about us."

Her stomach sunk to her designer heels. Why did he have to bring up that subject now? Had he been able to read her thoughts?

"Now's not a good time." She pulled her hand away from his, hoping the distance would clear her thoughts. "I just realized that we don't have long until the interview." She pushed aside the rest of her breakfast, having lost her appetite.

"Go ahead and finish eating. We have time."

She shook her head as she washed down the eggs and toast with a big sip of juice. "I want to be early. We need enough time to cover everything without rushing." She lifted her trusty black leather notepad from the table. "I have a lot of questions planned."

"And what would you like me to do?"

"Don't forget to record the session. I don't want to miss anything. You downloaded the app to your phone, didn't you?"

He nodded. "And don't forget to get her to authorize the recording."

"I have the legal release with my questions." She felt like she was forgetting something. "Was there anything else?"

Trey paused as though to go over everything in his mind. "Not that I can think of. Are you ready to go?"

She nodded. "You know, as much walking as we do, I need to start wearing sneakers and carrying my heels in a backpack."

"Do you want to change?"

She was very tempted, but she also knew they weren't the only ones trekking around Cannes. She needed to look her best at all times—or at least until she secured a few more interviews. Maybe after those she could let down her hair so to speak.

The sunny streets of Cannes were filled with some of the best-dressed people in the world. There were actors and actresses from action movies, romantic comedies and dramas. After almost a week of this, he was getting a lot more adept at matching names with faces. He wouldn't admit it here, but he wasn't much of a moviegoer. He was probably the only one in this large mass of people.

He walked with Sage back to the hotel where the Red Heart Gala had been held—where they'd kissed. He wondered if Sage was remembering their steamy lip-lock.

He'd never had a chance to explain why he'd pulled away. There'd always been a reason why it hadn't been the right time, but the truth was he'd been dragging his feet—delaying the inevitable.

In the elevator, he turned to her. "After the interview, we'll have that talk."

Her gaze averted his. "Okay."

Soon the truth would be out there and it wouldn't be weighing on him. He just didn't know how Sage would react. Would she understand that in the beginning he hadn't set out to hurt anyone?

His thoughts ground to a halt as they stepped off the elevator and approached the suite.

Trey knocked on the door.

There was no answer.

He glanced at Sage. "This is the right suite, isn't it?"

She referenced her notes. "It's the room number she gave me. Try again."

He knocked once more, louder this time.

At last the door swung open. A frazzled-looking young woman peeked her head through the crack in the door. This was not the actress. It must be her assistant. The woman's gaze moved from him to Sage and then back to him. She wasn't exactly the friendliest assistant as she had yet to say a word to them.

"Hi." He used his friendliest smile in spite of her. "Miss White is here for her interview with Starr."

"That won't be possible." The young woman attempted to close the door in Trey's face.

He was too quick for her and put his shoe in the way, bringing the swinging door to an abrupt halt. "Not so fast."

The young woman glared at him. "Move."

"Not until you tell us what is going on here. Miss White has an appointment."

"Yeah, well, things have changed. The appointment is canceled."

Sage stepped around Trey. "I don't understand. The other day Starr was anxious for the interview. Why did she change her mind?"

The young woman glanced over her shoulder as though to see if anyone was listening. "She's just signed an exclusive contract to sell her biography to be released simultaneously with her movie next year. All her promo is now monitored."

"But our agreement was prior to her contract." Sage had the look on her face that said she wasn't going to back down easily.

There were voices inside. The voices were growing louder as if they were approaching the door. Before he saw her, Trey knew the source of the problem.

The door swung wide open and Elsa appeared. She smiled but it wasn't a normal smile. It held a hint of deviousness. And her dark eyes sparkled with evil. The woman gave him a bitter taste in the back of his mouth. All he wanted to do was get Sage far away from the woman.

"Come on," he said. "Let's go."

"Yes, go." There was a note of glee in Elsa's voice. "There is nothing for you here."

Sage's face hardened. Her gaze narrowed in on her stepmother. "You had absolutely no interest in Starr until you knew I had plans with her."

"You did?" Elsa pressed a hand to her chest and feigned an innocent look. "Oh, my." The over-the-top theatrics made it obvious that Elsa had been targeting Sage. "You should pack up and go home."

Trey went to step up to the woman and let her know exactly what he thought of her. Words popped into his mind that he never thought he would ever say to a lady, but then again Elsa was anything but a lady.

Sage grabbed his arm and held him back. She glanced at him with a warning reflected in her eyes. "I've got this." She turned on Elsa. "I don't know why you think you have to lash out at me at every turn. You know, I feel bad for you."

"Bad for me?" Elsa's eyes widened in surprise. "Honey, I'm the one that is about to walk away with this year's up-and-coming superstar. You should feel bad for yourself—always on the losing end of things."

"I might not have gotten the interview, but I have something more—my self-respect and the ability to smile. You, however, don't even know what it's like to be happy. Do you?"

Frown lines bracketed Elsa's face. If looks could kill, Sage would be nothing but a black singe on the red carpet. "Oh, yes. You think you can stand up to me now that you have Quentin by your side. But even he is no challenge for me."

"His name is Trey."

"Really? My mistake." Elsa's voice took on a deeper, more deadly tone. "Or perhaps it's yours. You always were the naive child, wanting Daddy to take care of everything."

Sage turned to him. "Trey, tell her." There was pleading in her eyes that tore at him. "Tell her she's mistaken."

He wanted to do that for Sage. He would have done anything to spare Sage this agonizing moment, but it was now out of his hands. It was long past the time for the truth.

As the pain reflected in Sage's eyes, Trey's chest tightened. Every muscle in his body grew rigid. Everything with Sage was spinning out of control and he was helpless to stop it. He, the man with all the answers, didn't know how to keep Sage from being hurt.

He turned to Elsa.

How could one woman be so evil? So malicious?

The look of triumph sparkled in Elsa's eyes. His hands clenched at his sides. Why did she want to hurt her stepdaughter so badly?

The last thing he was going to let the woman do was stick around so she could gloat. "You've done your damage, now crawl back to whatever rock you slithered out from under."

She smiled at him, making his skin crawl. Elsa stepped up to him. She gave his body a lingering glance. "Aren't you a feisty one? We could have a good time together."

"Go."

Elsa sighed. "Such a pity." She moved on to Sage. "This isn't over."

"I didn't think it was." Sage lifted her chin. "We are just getting started."

Elsa let out an evil cackle. "We'll see about that." She glanced back at Trey. "As for you, Quentin Thomas Rousseau III, I'm not sure you're as much of a challenge as your father."

His gaze sought out Sage. Her eyes reflected the shock and disbelief. He wished he could tell her that Elsa was lying, but he couldn't. Elsa had done what he should have done long ago.

Sage's mouth opened but no words came out. Her gaze moved from Elsa to him.

"Oops. There I go again, letting that cat out of

the bag." A toothy grin lit up the woman's face. "I'm sure you two must have things to discuss."

Elsa cackled as she swept past them and headed for the bank of elevators. Trey waited until Elsa was out of earshot before he said, "Sage, I can explain."

It was too late. The damage was done. It was written all over Sage's beautiful face. The disappointment and distrust reflected in her eyes sliced through his heart.

"I don't even know what to call you anymore. Quentin? Thomas? Trey?"

Trey stood tall, ready to face what he'd done. "You can call me Trey. It was my nickname in boarding school."

"Fine. Trey, I have just one question." Her shiny gaze never wavered from his.

He already knew the question, but he wouldn't take away her right to ask it. He owed her that much and more.

"Go ahead." He thought he was ready for her words. He was tough. He was used to facing life alone. And he never thought this relationship, whatever title you wanted to hang on it, would last.

Sage leveled her shoulders and lifted her chin. "Was everything we shared a lie? Were you secretly laughing when I opened up about my past?"

That wasn't the question he'd been anticipating. He thought she'd want him to confirm that he was indeed Quentin Thomas Rousseau III. But she'd jumped ahead. She was already questioning everything they'd ever shared.

"No. It wasn't a lie."

"And the château? Is it yours?"

"Yes."

"Everything was a lie."

"No, it wasn't. Please believe me."

"I don't."

As he looked into her eyes, he could see that he'd already lost her. She'd already closed him off and relegated him to the list of people in her life that had hurt and betrayed her.

The guilt piled on him. He needed to say so much, but before he could figure out where to begin, Sage turned her back on him, and with her chin held high, she walked away.

He'd hurt the kindest, most generous person he'd ever known. He didn't deserve to be forgiven, but he wanted her forgiveness as much as he needed oxygen.

How did he convince her that these growing feelings were very real indeed—more so than he'd ever thought possible?

CHAPTER TWELVE

SHE WOULD NOT look over her shoulder.

She would not.

Sage's heart ached as she walked away from Trey or Quentin or whatever he wanted to call himself. She'd thought at last she found someone that she could trust. Someone that would be a true friend. She couldn't have been more wrong.

Why hadn't she seen it? It was all right there in front of her if she'd had been thinking with her head instead of her heart.

There was his Rolex watch. That was no knock-off. It was the genuine article. And now that she thought of it, he did bear a slight resemblance to his father. And there were his fine clothes including more than one tux. Those definitely didn't come from a secondhand shop like her red gown.

The elevator deposited her on the ground floor. She didn't waste any time heading for the door. She should shove aside all these tangled emotions and work. It was her reason for being in France. But the lump in her throat would keep her from speaking to anyone.

She walked straight out the front door and kept walking with no particular destination in mind. All the while, she continued to think of the telltale signs of his deception. His résumé, it had been too perfect. She wondered which things he had told her were the truth and which were the lies. She shook her head. No, she didn't want to know. It'd only make it worse.

The more she thought of Trey, the faster she walked. Her vision blurred, but she blinked it back into focus. Why in the world had she thought he would be different?

Here she was trying to report on facts for the magazine and she couldn't even get the facts right in her own life. If people knew how gullible she was, they would never trust anything she published. And she couldn't blame them.

Trey probably laughed behind her back, thinking how easily he'd been able to deceive her. But why do it? Why try to fool her?

That last question dogged her the rest of the way back to the château. She tried every conceivable answer, but none of them made sense. What did he hope to accomplish by playing the part of her assistant?

She shook her head, trying to chase away the taunting questions. She had other matters that needed her attention. Once in her room, she grabbed her phone and started calling every hotel in Cannes. With the festival in full swing, she was hoping that there would be an early checkout.

Call after call, she learned there were no rooms

in Cannes…anywhere. She sighed. She didn't want to give up on her plans for the magazine. She was running out of time before the next board meeting where she had to present her plan for the restructure and sustainability of the magazine.

She needed caffeine. It would make her feel better. And maybe some chocolate. But first the coffee.

She had just reached the bottom of the stairs when Trey came through the door. His face was drawn and his hair was scattered as though he'd been raking his fingers through it. Was it wrong that she took some comfort in the fact that he was unhappy that his plan had been ruined?

His gaze met hers. "Sage, we need to talk."

"I think we said everything we need to say." She turned to head to the back of the house. And then on second thought, she turned back to Trey. "There is one thing."

"What's that?"

"You're fired."

With the tiniest bit of satisfaction, she turned and walked away. She still didn't understand his motive. She knew Elsa was not above blackmail or other devious motives. But Sage just couldn't believe Elsa was behind Trey's actions. She'd seen Trey's reaction to Elsa. They definitely weren't working together.

So what was going on?

* * *

Fired.

As he watched her walk away, the word echoed in Trey's mind. It was a first for him. Having been his own boss since college, he'd never been in this position. And even though he was the CEO, the fact that Sage felt the need to fire him pricked his ego.

But what was bothering him most of all was the fact that he'd hurt her. Sage had been nothing but good to him. Looking back now, he realized his excuses for not telling her were because he knew once the truth was out there that Sage wouldn't look at him the same way.

He hadn't wanted to lose the close connection that they'd developed. It was new and fragile. It was a connection unlike any other he'd ever experienced in his life.

He should go after Sage. If the problem festered, there would be absolutely no chance for him to repair the damage. He still wasn't sure they could ever recapture what they had. Which was what?

They worked well together, but this thing between them went deeper. But how deep? He wasn't the commitment type. He supposed he'd gotten that from his father.

He didn't want to end up in a relationship like his parents. They never divorced, but they never lived together after his father walked away. He never understood why they'd remained married. What was the point of marriage?

He gave himself a mental shake. He didn't want to get caught up in the ghosts of the past. Right now, he had enough problems in the present. When it came to Sage, nothing was easy. And now he had to make amends—no, he *wanted* to make amends. There was definitely a difference between the two.

He started walking. He didn't know what he was going to say to her. Was there anything he could say that would convince her that they could still work together until the end of the festival? The fact that she was still at the château had to be a good sign, right? And then he remembered the festival and the lack of accommodations. It worked out for him.

At last, he caught up to her on the patio. "Sage. We need to talk."

She didn't even turn to look at him when she said, "We've said everything. There's nothing left to say."

"You might have said everything, but I didn't." He moved to stand in front of her. She averted her gaze, but that wouldn't deter him. "Sage, I'm sorry. I never meant to hurt you."

Her gaze met his. "What did you think was going to happen when you deceived me? That I'd never find out?"

"In the beginning, I didn't even consider how my plan might hurt others. I was after information and working as your assistant was the best way to gain unbiased information. I never factored in the people I'd be working with."

He could see the wheels of her mind spinning. "What information?"

"Can we sit down and talk?" He didn't want to make it easy for her to walk away when she heard something she didn't like.

Sage hesitated. Then she made her way over to a bench. "I don't know why I'm doing this."

"Because you need answers. You want to know why a CEO would go undercover in his own company."

"I do. So tell me. But don't think it will change anything between us." There was a firmness in her voice.

He knew it would take more than this talk in order for Sage to forgive him. But it was a start and that had to be enough...for now.

"Let me start at the beginning. How much do you know about my father and the trouble he got the magazine into?"

She shrugged. "Not a whole lot."

And so Trey revealed to her how his father had in recent years gone with the easy, sensational headlines and played it loose with the truth. And he'd gotten away with it until he started writing a string of fabricated stories about Deacon Santoro. The movie star had threatened a lawsuit that would put the whole corporation in jeopardy. At last, they settled out of court for a nominal amount and the removal of Trey's father from the business, but the settlement also included changing the editorial content. And that's where Sage came into the story.

"That explains the past, but it doesn't tell me why you entered my life," Sage said.

"With my father stepping down from the company, I was in line for the CEO position. It was my chance to do what I'd always wanted."

"What's that? Run the magazine? And I got in your way?"

Trey shook his head. "No. I never wanted any part of the magazine."

"But why?"

"Because it's all my father ever cared about. It wasn't me or my mother. It was *QTR*. And I just wanted him to know what it's like to lose something he loved."

Sage gasped. "You want to destroy *QTR* to get even with your father. But what about all the history? That magazine has been in your family for generations."

"Seven generations to be exact. I am the seventh heir. And I thought the last."

"You thought? You've changed your mind?" There was a note of hope in her voice.

He turned to look directly into her eyes. "You are a very passionate woman. When you get excited out about something, it shows in your face, your voice—it's infectious."

"And that's how you now feel about the magazine?" Suspicion reflected in her eyes.

"I didn't at first. I thought you were crazy for wanting to save that dying rag. I couldn't imagine what you saw in the magazine to drive you to save it."

"And now?" Though the glint of suspicion still showed in her eyes, there was also the spark of curiosity.

"And then I started working with you. It was then that I saw what the magazine could be—what good it could do."

"This all sounds too convenient. Why should I believe you?"

"You shouldn't. Not after what I've done. But I wanted you to know that you opened my eyes to the potential of *QTR*."

"And if the future of the magazine were just up to you?"

"I'd continue to help you rebuild it. But it's not up to me. I'm just one vote on the board. And there is some staunch opposition."

"I guess you'd know since you were one of them."

He nodded. There was no denying it. "But if my mind can be changed, so can theirs."

"But not without a plan for the upcoming year.

I need a solid production schedule. And now between the bad reputation of the magazine and Elsa's conniving, I don't have anyone on the calendar."

"You still have time."

"No, I don't. I'm leaving tomorrow. I'm flying back to California and putting this whole miserable experience behind me."

The thought that he caused her to give up hurt him more than he thought possible. He refused to give up—on the magazine and especially on setting things right with Sage.

"Don't go." The words passed his lips before he could think through the ramifications.

"Why? So you can lie to me some more?"

"I'm not lying to you. Things can never be the same again, but I will prove to you that I can do better—that you can trust me."

"With us being on opposite sides of the magazine?"

"I told you I've changed my mind."

"And you expect me to just believe you? Would you have ever told me the truth if Elsa hadn't outed you?"

He lowered his head. "I tried to tell you several times. There was always a convenient excuse to put it off. It just never seemed like the right time. We were getting along so well and I… I didn't want to ruin what we had."

"You certainly did that."

He scratched at his beard. "I know. And I'm sorry."

"At least your father must be happy that you changed your mind about the magazine."

"He doesn't know."

"But why not?"

"My father and I aren't close. In fact—" he paused because it still hurt for him to admit "—I don't know him at all."

"You don't?"

He shook his head. "My father left my mother when I was three years old. He said he couldn't run his magazine from France."

"Why didn't your mother go with him?"

"She said her life was in France. And that she would never fit into his world any more than he fit into hers."

"That's so sad."

Trey shrugged. "I think there was more to the story, but my mother died before she told me the whole truth. She didn't like talking about my father."

"It must have been tough being the child of divorced parents."

"That's the thing, they never divorced. In fact, my father showed up at my mother's funeral. He tried to reach out to me but I told him it was too little, too late."

"And that's it? You haven't spoken to him since?"

Trey turned to Sage. "Why do you sound so surprised?"

"It's just that any time your father spoke of you, he always had such glowing reports."

"He talked about me?" Trey found that hard to believe.

Anxious to turn the spotlight off himself, Trey realized this was his chance to learn more about Sage. "How do you know my father?"

"We initially met when I interned for him during the summer of my junior and senior years of college."

"You must have made quite an impression on my father."

She shrugged. "I'm not so sure it was that as much as he thought when he hired me that he would be able to control me."

Trey smiled. "I'm guessing you set him straight."

"I did. And he wasn't too happy about it, but by then there was nothing he could do." She turned to him. "But he does care about you. Remember those photos of you and your mother? He really did keep them on his desk. A person doesn't do that unless they care."

Trey shook his head. "He doesn't. I can assure you of that. He made it clear when he left."

Sage reached out and placed her hand over his. "I don't know what went wrong between your parents, but I'm telling you he never stopped caring about you. Maybe you should talk to him. Hear his side—"

"No." Trey got to his feet. "That isn't going to happen."

"I don't have to tell you that if you pass up this chance, you might not get another. I lost both of my parents and you lost your mother. This is your chance to get answers."

Trey turned to her. He didn't know how things had gotten so turned around. He was supposed to be apologizing for his deception, but somehow they were now delving into his past. And he had to put a stop to it.

"I don't need answers." There was absolutely no hesitation in his voice. "I don't want that man in my life. I'm fine on my own."

Her gaze studied him for a moment and then there was a glint of sympathy. "Everyone needs somebody."

The truth poked at his heart, but he refused to acknowledge it. "What about you? I don't see you going out of your way to draw people into your life."

"Really? Are you so sure about that?"

He paused. That wasn't the answer he'd been expecting. Where was she going with it?

He pressed his hand to his sides. "Okay. Who have you let into your life?"

She arched a fine brow. "You, for starters."

It was true. She had let him in. She'd told him about her past and about Elsa. She'd shared so much with him and he'd let her down.

"And there are my roommates, Lisa and Ann. Louise, at the office, is like a mother hen. And I've gotten to know everyone at the office. We're like one big, dysfunctional family."

Everything she'd said was true. Because it wasn't the traditional sense of a family, he hadn't recognized it as such. But she was right; she took what she had and made a support system for herself. It was more than he had done. Suddenly he felt so alone in this world—it was a staggering moment—much like what he'd felt at his mother's funeral.

And when they left Cannes, he knew Sage would return to her makeshift family with their laughter, teasing and closeness. He, on the other hand, would return to San Francisco where he spent hours in solitude working on his newest security software. And when he was at the office, people kept their distance because he was the boss—not a boss like Sage.

And there was his father. His father might mistakenly think Trey's change of mind about the magazine meant he changed his mind about him, but nothing could be farther from the truth. His father would never again have anything to do with the magazine or QTR International.

If Trey had his way, Sage would stay on as managing editor. But would she agree after what she'd learned?

His gaze met hers. "I just wanted to tell you that I'm sorry. I never meant for things to work out like they have."

And with that he turned and walked away. Too much had been said that evening. He needed to clear his head. Those things Sage had said about his father...they couldn't be right. His father had more than thirty years to be a part of his life and he hadn't done it. Perhaps he'd just been putting on a show for people.

Sage was such an optimist. He knew she wanted him to have a relationship with his father—something she would never have again. But she had to understand that their fathers were very different men. It was never going to happen for him.

CHAPTER THIRTEEN

WHAT TO DO?

After a restless night, Sage was up early. Her conversation with Trey kept rolling around in her mind. Logic told her not to believe him—that he wasn't to be trusted. But her heart said the feelings and emotions they'd shared had been genuine.

Her phone buzzed. She glanced at the caller ID, finding it was her private investigator. She immediately answered. "Have you learned something?"

"I'm on to something big," the man said.

"Tell me."

"It's not complete and I want to be sure before I give you the information. It might take me extra time. Are the added fees going to be a problem?"

Yes. She was giving him every single cent aside from her rent and food. She thought of the money she was going to use to fly home early. The airline wouldn't switch the return portion of her ticket and so she'd have to purchase a new one. But in the light of day, things with Trey didn't appear so dire. If she stayed, it'd save a lot of money.

"Miss White?"

"No. It won't be a problem." She needed answers and she'd do whatever it took to get them.

"Okay. I need a few more details and then I'll

give you everything I've collected. I think it's what you're after."

And then a thought came to Sage. Part of her told her not to do it, but a louder voice in her head said it was better to know the truth. "Did you uncover any information regarding Trey...er... Quentin Thomas Rousseau III being involved with Elsa?"

"No. He's not."

The answer came so quickly that it surprised her. "Are you sure?"

"One hundred percent positive."

It didn't get any more certain. "Thanks. Keep digging into Elsa's past. There's something there that she doesn't want us to know about." And with any luck it would be the key to Sage regaining her legacy.

She ended the call knowing that staying here with Trey or Quentin or whatever he wanted to call himself wouldn't be easy. Could she avoid him? Not likely since they were sharing the house. There had to be some way to coexist for a little longer.

Trey refilled his coffee for the fourth time the next morning.

He'd tossed and turned most of the night. Before sunrise, he'd climbed out of bed. He needed to think about something besides how bad he'd screwed things up with Sage.

A glance in the bathroom mirror showed proof

of his bad night. But as he scratched at the irritating beard, he realized there was nothing stopping him from shaving. In fact, there was no reason not to put in his contacts. At last, he could get back to being himself. Although there were a couple of changes he wanted to keep—his nickname and the shorter hair.

After his shower and shave, Trey paced back and forth in the kitchen in his bare feet while a new pot of coffee brewed. He yawned and stretched. It'd been a long time since he'd pulled an all-nighter.

"Mind if I come in?"

The sound of Sage's voice had him turning. "Sure. You don't have to ask. You are always welcome."

She openly stared at him.

Had he nicked himself shaving? "What's wrong?"

"You. I mean, you look so different." She continued gazing at him. "Is this how you normally look when you're not pretending to be an assistant?"

"I am sorry about that." He could tell by the stony look in her eyes that his apology didn't sway her. "Yes, this is me except for the hair. I used to wear it longer, much longer. But I'm liking this shorter style. It's a lot easier to deal with. What do you think?"

She shrugged and moved past him toward the freshly brewed coffee. She poured herself a cupful. He noticed that she didn't offer to get him any. It was to be expected.

He wondered what it'd take to get them past this awkward spot. There had to be a way because the future of the magazine was at stake. But more than that, he wouldn't let Sage lose and Elsa win.

Now, he had to prove to Sage that they made a great team and together they could fend off Elsa. "We're going to have to work together if we're going to defeat Elsa."

"This is my fight." Her voice was firm.

"It's our fight. Yours and mine."

She gave him a strange look. "Why would you take on my stepmother?"

"You mean besides the fact that I hate the way she treats you?"

Sage nodded.

It was time he laid out the truth—a truth that even he found surprising. "Because of you, I have found an appreciation for *QTR*." Her eyes widened but she remained quiet and so he continued. "You've shown me what it could be. I like the idea of using it to show the good parts of life. The news these days is so full of depressing topics that I'd like to be a part of showing the world the positive side of life. And I'm thinking my ancestors would have liked the idea of their magazine being an instrument for good."

"You mean there's something good that has come from all of this?"

"If you're referring to my attitude toward keeping the magazine, then yes."

"And then you can hand it down to your son—"

"No, that isn't going to happen. I'm not going to put a child through what I experienced growing up."

"You don't need to. I've known both you and your father. Yes, there are some similarities but you are very different people. I could see you being a loving, involved father—"

"Sage, stop. It isn't going to happen. I want to see the magazine survive. Nothing more."

A frown settled on her face.

"Stop looking at me like I just ran over your teddy bear."

"It's not you. It's just that the future of the magazine isn't up to me or you. There's the board to contend with and I have a meeting with them at the end of the month to determine whether the magazine continues or is closed down. And right now, I do not have a compelling calendar to show them. If I don't get some big names to grace the covers, they'll be sure to close us."

"You forget that I'm the CEO. I have sway over that board. We'll compile a winning calendar of interviews. And as for Elsa, we'll beat her at her own game."

"How? I thought about it all night and haven't come up with anything except locking her in her hotel room. Or better yet, stuffing her in a suitcase and putting her in the cargo hold of the first plane bound for the States."

Trey laughed. "I didn't know you had such a devious mind."

Sage still didn't smile when she said, "Oh, trust me. I have my moments."

"Anything you care to share?"

"Not yet."

Well, he had to admit that he was intrigued now. There was so much more to Sage than her sunny smile and friendly personality. Beneath her beauty was a strong businesswoman that wasn't afraid to go after what she wanted. He was looking forward to this battle with Sage by his side.

But the most important thing to him was putting the smile back on Sage's face. He had stolen it away and that acknowledgment dug at him. If it was the last thing he did, he would make Sage happy again—even if it meant exiting her life after *QTR* was secure.

He was going to step up his game.

He was no longer an observer.

Trey had signed on to fight for the magazine and that meant thinking outside the box.

They'd just finished watching the premiere of a

French film that made a statement about caring for those with mental health issues. It was very powerful. He wondered if Sage knew the language or if she was taking advantage of the subtitles. He wouldn't know because their communication so far that day had pertained to business only—nothing personal.

Outside the theater, a mass of photographers were snapping more photos of the stars. One photographer told Trey and Sage to pose. She didn't want to, but Trey coaxed her into it. He casually placed his arm around her waist. He longed to pull her closer, but he resisted the urge.

As soon as the photo was taken, Sage pulled away. She immediately set to work talking to any performer who would listen to her.

The more he observed her, the more he knew that there was no stopping her. Just like now, as they stood outside the theater, she was doing her best to make connections. One by one, people turned away from her. Trey wanted to go up to them and tell them to quit being so rude, but he knew Sage wouldn't appreciate the gesture nor would it help their situation.

Sage was a strong woman who didn't need anyone to take care of her. Her strength and determination impressed him. She didn't turn the magazine around with backdoor deals. She didn't pay people off. She didn't make outrageous promises. She did absolutely nothing wrong.

Sage turned the magazine around with integrity, smarts and kindness.

Kindness. Who would have figured?

She was kind to people, found out what they were passionate about and then agreed to get on board to further their pet projects. It was a win-win for everyone.

Now how did you stop something that was so good?

"Trey, this isn't working." Sage frowned. "Everyone sees the name of my publication and turns away. Or worse, they tell me what they think of *QTR*. And it's nothing I would repeat. Maybe I should propose to the board that we take on a new name."

Trey shook his head. "The reputation my father put upon the magazine will follow you, even through a name-change."

"Then maybe I should take off my badge. At least then people will give me a chance before they reject what I'm offering."

"You need your badge to give you access to the festival events, but…" He paused to give this some thought.

"But what?"

She'd been on to something. He just needed to think for a moment.

"Trey. Speak."

"Maybe you need a different approach."

"You mean instead of being up front about the magazine I represent?" When he nodded, she said, "Even though it's clearly printed on my press badge?"

He hadn't gotten this far in business without cutting some corners or playing a little subterfuge. If people got to know Sage without the curse of *QTR* hanging around her neck, both literally and figuratively, they would see that she would never sink to the level of his father.

And then he realized what they needed to do. He looked at the worried expression on her face and couldn't wait to replace it with one of her bright, contagious smiles.

"Come with me." And without thinking, he took her hand in his.

Her hand felt good wrapped around his. It was like they were two pieces of a puzzle and they fit together. He made a point of zigzagging through the crowd of smartly dressed people.

When they'd cleared the crowd of people, Sage withdrew her hand. "Where are we going?"

"You'll see."

"I'd rather know. I really need to get back there and try to make some sort of connection, even if I have to hang a sign around my neck that says *QTR* has changed."

He smiled at her as he led her toward Cannes' elite shops. "You're on the right track."

"I am?" She sent him a puzzled look. "We're going to make a sign?"

He chuckled. "Nothing quite so obvious."

"Now you have me intrigued. What exactly are you up to?"

"I told you, you'll see soon enough. Just enjoy the sunshine and the walk." He resisted the urge to take her hand back in his.

Soon they arrived at the shopping area. Now he just had to find the right shop.

"If you would tell me what you're searching for, I could help."

At that moment, he spotted it. "No need. I found it."

They crossed the street and approached the exclusive jewelry store. "We're here."

"Here?" Sage glanced at the showroom window and then back at him. "You want to go jewelry shopping now?"

He shrugged. "It seemed like a good idea at the time. Come on. Let's have a look inside."

Without waiting for her to protest, he opened the door for her. Sage hesitated, but eventually she stepped forward.

He knew what he was looking for. He passed by the gemstones, the sparkling diamond rings and the designer watches. And then he stopped in front of a glass case.

A young woman with a blond ponytail and navy

blue dress stepped up to them. "Is there something I can show you?"

Sage leaned closer and whispered, "What are you doing?"

"Trust me." He stared in the brightly lit glass case. His gaze skimmed past gold chains and paused at a bunch of large pendants. There were flowers, animals and other artistic shapes. "What's your favorite color?"

"Red. A deep wine red."

He glanced around until he found a silver filigree flower pendant that was accented with rubies. It was large and it was beautiful. It would do.

He pointed to it. "That one."

The young woman removed it from the case. "Would you like to try it on?"

He gave Sage a quick glance. She was still frowning at him. He turned back to the saleswoman. "That's okay. We'll take it."

With a frustrated sigh, Sage turned for the door.

He knew in this type of store that prices wouldn't be marked on the jewelry. You didn't come in here unless you could afford the precious gems. And right now, he'd pay anything to make things right with Sage. But he knew this necklace wouldn't buy him forgiveness. It wasn't why he'd purchased it.

Once he'd paid for the necklace, he joined Sage on the sidewalk. "I was worried you wouldn't wait for me."

"If you bought that for me, take it back. You should spend your money on someone you care about."

"I care about you." The words popped out before he could stop them. Was that true? Did he care about her? Now wasn't the time to evaluate his emotions. He had to correct his slipup. "You know I care about you getting the magazine turned around."

She continued to look at him as though not sure she believed him. Finally, she glanced away. "You know you can't put that through on an expense report, right?"

"I know. It'll be fine. Trust me." He reached inside the fancy bag and withdrew the black velvet box. "Let's try this on."

Sage continued to mutter about how foolish this was, but once the necklace was on her, she quieted down. "It covers part of my badge."

"The important part. The magazine's name."

She sent him a puzzled look, which was quickly replaced with a smile. "You want people to notice the necklace instead of the name of our magazine."

"Exactly. First impressions are so important. There's time later for telling them that you represent *QTR*."

She smiled at him. "I knew there was a reason I hired you."

"As I recall, I predicted you would hire me because I was the best."

"The best, huh?"

For a moment, things were easy and fun between them. And the way she smiled at him made him want to lean in and kiss her. He knew that wasn't possible, but it didn't make him desire her any less.

He cleared his throat. "We should get back to the festival and see if this beauty helps you land an interview or two."

"Or three," she added. As they started to walk side by side, she said, "I'll pay you back for this."

He didn't say anything, not wanting to ruin this moment of easiness. He'd missed the laughing, smiling Sage more than he thought possible. This was a start, he just had to build on it—show her that she wasn't wrong about him.

CHAPTER FOURTEEN

SAGE FINGERED THE beautiful pendant.

It felt strange to be wearing a piece of jewelry purchased by Trey. She knew it was purely a strategic move and that there weren't any emotions tied to it. But every time she looked at it, her heart beat faster.

"Hey, where'd you go?" Trey stared at her across an umbrella table where they'd been enjoying a light lunch.

"I was just thinking I shouldn't be sitting here. I should be circulating and putting your plan to work."

"You don't have to push yourself every minute of the day. Sometimes you need to just enjoy yourself."

"I will once I accomplish what I came here to do."

He looked at her like he didn't believe her. "You've accomplished a lot in the short amount of time since you've been at *QTR*."

"And there's so much more to do." Her gaze moved over his shoulder, landing on an A-list actress. Her last two movies had been box office hits.

Trey pulled up the notes he'd made about the actress's past films, upcoming ventures and interests.

He read off the information to Sage. Armed with the information to make this hopefully a successful conversation, Sage stood up.

"Good luck," he said. "If you don't need me, I'm going to do some mingling. I'll text you if I get something."

Her gaze kept straying back to the actress, making sure she didn't get away. When she glanced back at Trey, she said, "I'll see you back at the château."

She moved away quickly to catch up with the actress.

You can do this. They'll like your idea. You just have to get them to listen.

"Hi." Sage smiled as she approached the young woman. "Aren't you Abigail Wright from the movie *Visitors from Beyond*?"

"Why, yes, I am." The young woman smiled at being recognized from one of the films being played here at the festival. "Did you enjoy it?"

"I did."

They went on to discuss the film for a couple of minutes. Perhaps Trey had been right about the beautiful piece of jewelry. So far it had been her lucky charm.

The actress's gaze strayed to Sage's badge, which was still obscured by the pendant. "I see you are with the press."

"I am. And I would love to interview you." She

was thankful Trey had researched the actress's professional background as well as her volunteer work. "I know you've done some volunteering to build houses for those less fortunate."

The actress's face lit up. "I have. It's a really great venture."

"Perhaps we could frame the interview around the volunteer work you've done and then segue into your films."

"I would like that. What outlet are you with?"

This was the moment of truth. *"QTR Magazine."*

The young woman paused and Sage prayed she wouldn't change her mind about the interview. At last, the actress gave Sage her contact information and they agreed to a time and location.

Sage couldn't tell if the actress was too new to the business to know about the scandalous past of *QTR* or if she was so hungry for attention that she didn't care. Either way, it had worked out for Sage.

One interview down, more to go. And it was thanks to Trey. He was the one that thought of the lovely piece of jewelry to camouflage her true identity. She hoped one day soon those tactics wouldn't be necessary. She wanted *QTR Magazine* to be synonymous with integrity. But for now, Trey had earned a few points in his favor.

Sage adjusted the pendant over her pink press badge, straightened her shoulders and lifted her chin. Steadily putting one foot in front of the other, she headed for the group of people gathered outside the Debussy Theatre.

She worked the crowd like a pro. Agents exchanged business cards with Sage, giving her a sense of optimism. No, it wasn't a firm date for an interview, but each card represented an open door. And she planned to march through those doors.

She'd just approached Johnny Volt, an action movie superstar, when Elsa materialized out of nowhere. Trying to ignore her stepmother's looming presence, Sage said, "It's so nice to meet you."

Sage and Johnny shook hands and exchanged pleasantries.

This was her chance to turn this casual conversation into something more productive. "Mr. Volt—"

"Please, call me Johnny."

"Okay. Johnny, I've heard a lot about your movie releasing in August. It's projected to be a box office hit just like the first one. I was wondering if you'd be interested in a magazine cover and a feature article."

"What magazine are you with?"

"Excuse me." Elsa took that moment to interrupt. "I'm Elsa."

Sage smothered a groan. She would not give Elsa the satisfaction of seeing how her interruption bothered her. Still, it annoyed Sage how the woman descended upon them mid-conversation and announced her name like she was one of those celebrities that only went by their first name. Did she really think she was that big of a name?

"If you'll excuse us," Sage said in a restrained tone, "we were in the middle of a conversation."

Elsa turned back to Johnny. "Before you agree to anything with *QTR*, you'll want to hear what I can offer you. It'll far surpass anything they can do."

Johnny glanced at Elsa with disdain. "You heard her. We're talking. Privately. Now if you'll excuse us."

Elsa's deep-red lips gaped. It would appear that she was not used to being dismissed. Sage struggled to keep from laughing at the horrified expression on Elsa's face when Johnny turned his back to her.

"Is she gone yet?"

With a loud sigh, Elsa turned on her five-inch heels and walked away.

"She is now." Sage stopped herself from apologizing for her stepmother. In the past, that's exactly what she would have done. But not now. She may share her last name with the woman, but she wasn't family. And Elsa's actions were no reflection on her.

"I would like to hear more about what you have to offer. Can I have your phone?" Johnny held out his hand.

She couldn't believe that *the* Johnny Volt was not only talking to her, but he was also going to put his number in her phone. With a slightly shaky hand, she gave him her phone.

He quickly typed in his information. "Give me a call next week and we'll set something up." He returned the phone. "But now I have to go. It was good to meet you."

After Johnny disappeared into the crowd, Trey approached her. "I saw Elsa and got concerned. What did I miss?"

"I'd say that good won out over evil."

Trey laughed. She loved the sound of his laugh. It was deep and warm. Her gaze caught and held his longer than necessary.

It would be so easy to forgive and forget, but she couldn't. She knew the price of trusting someone and then having them turn on you. Trey already proved he was someone she couldn't trust. She wouldn't make the same mistake again.

Using every bit of willpower, she glanced away. She refused to let down the wall around her heart. He'd already had his chance. That's all he got—but her heart didn't agree.

He had to do more.

The following afternoon, Trey had given a lot of thought to how he could make amends with Sage. He knew nothing he did would undo the past, but he wanted to show her he was better than that—he wanted to prove it to himself.

He'd let himself get so caught up in evening the score with his father that he hadn't realized the price it would exact from those around him.

He needed to get back to being himself.

He needed Sage to trust him again. And the pendant had been a start, but he wanted to do something extra special—something to put the spark back in Sage's big, beautiful eyes. And he had the inkling of an idea that just might do the trick. But he couldn't do it alone.

It was midway into the afternoon when Trey decided to make his departure. They had just arrived outside the Grand Theatre Lumière. The red carpet was in full action with celebrities in designer gowns, sparkling gems and black tuxes. When a celebrity stepped onto the carpet, camera flashes lit up the area. There were so many cameras that it was blinding.

Sage leaned close to him to speak over the crowd. "Did you see George? Oh, look, there's Uma. This movie is going to be amazing."

He loved hearing the enthusiasm in Sage's voice. Day by day, things were getting better between them. Though he wished the process was faster, he was grateful they'd made it this far.

He leaned close to her ear, catching the sweet scent of jasmine. He lingered for a moment, breathing in her intoxicating scent. When someone bumped into him, it jarred him back to his senses.

"Would you mind if I went back to the château for a bit?"

Concern filled Sage's eyes but in a blink it was gone. "Sure. I've got this. I got caught up in the fact that people are starting to talk with us. But when I mention an interview or a cover, they shy away."

"You'll nail it. Just give it time. The festival seems like a really big crowd, but it's really rather small when it comes to passing information. Once it gets around that you are so nice and have integrity, they will view *QTR* in a different light."

She looked at him with skepticism. "I don't know about that."

"Trust me." The words were out before he realized that was the exact wrong thing for him to say to her. "Forget that. Trust yourself and believe that you can do this."

As he walked away, he realized his campaign to win back Sage's friendship and perhaps her trust had to be many pronged. The first would be celebrating her birthday, which was quickly approaching. It landed on the next to the last day of the festival. And it wasn't going to be any birthday party. He had something very special in mind.

And the other idea was to deal with Elsa. He knew that Sage thought she could handle her, but he had to do something to help. That woman, she just couldn't get away with the way she treated Sage.

He would see about getting his group of online friends, aka hackers, to lend a hand. He'd never needed their help before, but they owed him for various things in the past. This was his time to collect. He needed to know everything about Elsa and all the things she didn't want other people to know—including her questionable acquisition of Sage's family company.

He strode quickly to the château. He needed to speak with Maria, his housekeeper, before she left for the day. She had been with him since he was a boy. In many ways, she was as much a mother to him as his own mother.

As soon as Trey entered the house, he headed for the kitchen. It was Maria's favorite room. She'd told him that numerous times over the years. And he had to agree with her. It was spacious, modern and had the most terrific view of the sea. It was one of the reasons he'd held on to the place.

"Maria." He entered the kitchen and came to a stop. He glanced all around, but she was nowhere to be found. "Maria?"

He started walking through the house looking for her. After covering the ground floor, he was starting to suspect she'd completed her work early and had gone home. He supposed he could phone her, but he'd rather go over the details in person.

He reached the top of the steps when the door to Sage's room opened. Maria stepped into the hallway. When her gaze caught him standing in the hallway, she jumped and pressed a hand to her chest.

When she spoke, it was in French. Though she also spoke English, she preferred her native language. "You startled me." She smiled at him. "I didn't know that anyone had returned."

"Sorry, it's just me."

"Can I get you anything?"

"I could really use your help."

Her eyes widened with interest. "Certainly. What do you need?"

"I need your help planning a birthday party for Sage. If you could take care of coordinating the food and staff, I'll take care of the invitations."

Maria smiled. "You really like her, don't you?"

He hesitated. Until now, he hadn't even admitted to himself about his growing feelings for Sage. For so long, he'd tried holding her at arm's length, but somewhere between rescuing Happy and the Red Heart Gala she'd broken through his barriers.

He wanted to believe that this was the beginning for them. He wanted to believe they could write a different story than the unhappy one his parents had lived.

"I... I do care about her. But I've really messed things up."

Maria patted his arm and sent him a sympathetic look. "Did you apologize?"

He nodded. "But it was more than an apology could cover."

"Give her time. Keep showing her that you care. She'll come around."

"I hope you're right."

"Of course I am. Who could resist that smile?" She patted his cheek. "Now, you'll need to give me a menu so I can get started shopping."

"About that, I have some very specific ideas to run by you."

Together they entered his office and they plotted out a birthday party that would be unlike any other.

CHAPTER FIFTEEN

THE FESTIVAL WAS nearing the end.

Late Thursday afternoon, Sage stared at her production calendar for the magazine; it still had noticeable gaps. For all their efforts, she still couldn't secure all the necessary interviews. And without a rock-solid plan, the board would vote against her. She was starting to wonder if this was a lost cause.

But if the magazine failed, it meant she wouldn't be able to keep up her payments to the private investigator. And she knew if he were taken off the case now, she would probably never get this close to uncovering Elsa's lies again.

And then there was Trey. She should be happy that the closing of the magazine meant he would be out of her life, but try as she did to dislike him—and she did try hard—there was something about him that made her want to forgive him. Had she forgiven him? Perhaps. But did she trust him? That was another story.

Knock. Knock.

"Come in." Sage looked up from the desk in her room.

The door swung open and Trey appeared. "I was wondering if you might be interested in an early dinner here at the château before we leave for the party."

"That sounds perfect. I just need to finish this email."

Trey nodded in understanding. "There's also something I'd like to discuss with you. Can you meet me downstairs when you're finished?"

She nodded and he left.

That was strange. She'd noticed the serious tone in his voice. In fact, his whole face wore a serious expression. What had happened? Or did he have another secret to reveal? Her heart sank. Was there something else he'd been lying to her about?

She turned back to her email, but it suddenly didn't seem like such a priority. She couldn't dismiss her worry. What if it wasn't Trey? What if Elsa was causing more problems?

Deciding she could finish the email later, she closed her laptop. She hurried downstairs. If her stepmother was causing problems for Trey, she would…she would do something. She just didn't know what that something would be. Messing with her was one thing, but messing with someone she cared about was quite another.

Sage came to a stop on the bottom step. Did she care about Trey? Her heart started to pound. The truth was she *did* care about him. She probably shouldn't, but her heart had won the battle over her head.

"Sage, there you are." Trey stepped in front of her. He didn't smile, not a good sign. "I thought you had an email to finish?"

"It can wait. This sounds serious."

"We can talk out on the veranda."

He waved for her to lead the way. She held her tongue until they were standing on the private balcony. But then she turned to him. "What is it? What has Elsa done now?"

His eyebrows rose. "How do you know it's her?"

Sage didn't but it was so much better than the alternative. "Call it intuition."

"Your intuition is right. I heard from one of our distributors today and they said they are discontinuing distribution of *QTR* to their supermarkets."

"What? But why?" And then realizing she already knew the answer to her own questions, she said, "Elsa. Of course. Did they say why?"

He shook his head. "They were very short and to the point. So I took it upon myself to make inquiries with a couple of our other distributors. It seems Elsa has been making the rounds."

Sage sat down before she fell down. Her whole world felt as though it were crumbling around her. "This can't be happening. That woman won't stop until she puts me in the ground. I probably wouldn't even die in a manner that would please her."

"Hey, it's not that dire. I was able to talk to all of the other distributors and keep them on board. So we're only down one."

"For now, until Elsa finds another way to stick it to me via the magazine." Now that the shock had worn off, anger was taking over. Sage got to her feet and started to pace. "If only I had a way to stop her."

"I might be able to help you."

"What? But how?"

"You know how I'm into computers and security software, right?" She nodded and he continued. "In my business, you get to know the best hackers because I need them to break into my software in order for me to make it stronger."

"So you hire criminals?"

"Pretty much. Hey, if the government can hire them, I can, too. It helps keep them out of trouble."

"But I have a feeling you've turned them back to their illegal activities."

"I'm not admitting anything. All I'll say is that I have a handful of trusted computer experts, and if there's anything in cyberspace to stop Elsa, they will find it. She has no idea what sort of war she has started." Trey looked so proud of himself that she hated to say anything. But he must have read it on her face. "What aren't you saying?"

She sighed. "I had someone do the internet thing and they couldn't turn up anything."

"They weren't looking in the dark corners these guys will be searching. I'm not saying they will, but they could look on her very own computer. That is, if they wanted to."

"I'm sure they will." She wanted to trust Trey. But he'd already let her down once. What would stop him from doing it again?

"Talk to me, Sage." The hopeful look faded from his face. He stepped up to her and reached out, taking her hands in his own. "I know I hurt you, but I promise it won't happen again. If we're going to beat Elsa, we have to work together."

He was right. They were stronger together. She'd been working on taking Elsa down by herself for the past year, but there still wasn't enough to make Elsa relinquish her hold on her family's company.

She stared deep into Trey's eyes. Inside her a war raged—to trust him or not. Having access to all of *QTR*'s files, he had the ability to hurt her. But he hadn't. Nor had he walked away after his cover was blown. He seemed genuinely interested in saving the magazine.

Maybe it was time to give him the benefit of the doubt.

Sage inhaled a deep steadying breath and then she slowly blew it out. "I also have someone digging into Elsa's web of lies. He uncovered small things, but nothing that would stand up in court and prove she didn't belong at White Publishing."

"This person, do you trust him?"

"Let's just say I trust him as much as I trust anyone who makes their living out of spying on people. So far he's proven himself reliable." Now for the latest development. "And he's on to something big."

Had she forgiven him?

It was so hard to tell.

Trey stood on the deck of the luxury yacht surrounded by celebrities in their finest attire, but he only had eyes for Sage. She was the only star in his eyes.

Her black clingy dress emphasized her curves and made it difficult to concentrate. And the thigh-high slit that gave him glimpses of her bare legs—

He halted his thoughts. He had to maintain a cool, nonchalant attitude. He couldn't risk making a move and scaring her off.

For the life of him, he couldn't read her. She said and did all the right things, but it still felt like there was a distance between them—a wall he wasn't able to scale. It made sense. Sage had been hurt repeatedly in the past. She had learned to armor herself. And he'd foolishly let her down. If only he could undo the past.

Trey forced a smile to his lips as he sidestepped the dancing couples and approached Sage. He carried an umbrella drink that all the guests were raving about. "Here you go. This drink comes highly recommended."

She accepted the orange drink topped with a pineapple chunk and a maraschino cherry. "Where's yours?"

He shook his head and held out his club soda. "I'm driving tonight."

"We didn't drive here. We hired a car, remember?"

He smiled. "I must have been distracted by this gorgeous brunette sitting next to me."

Sage arched a fine brow. "Are you flirting with me?"

"Do you want me to be?"

"That's not fair. You answered a question with a question." She sipped at her fruity drink. "Mmm… They are right. This is amazing."

"And you are changing the subject."

He turned away from all the people and stared out over the water as the Mediterranean sun hovered over the horizon splashing the sky with brilliant shades of orange and pink. Summer had come early to Cannes. And it felt good to be out here on this impressive yacht. Perhaps he'd purchase his own.

"It's a beautiful sunset, isn't it?" Sage asked.

He glanced her way. "Very beautiful indeed."

Her gaze caught his. "You weren't talking about the sunset, were you?"

"No, I wasn't." Suddenly feeling a bit warm, he downed the rest of the club soda.

Her big blue almost violet eyes stared up at him. He longed to pull her in his arms and kiss away all of her doubts. No other woman in his life—and there had been a number of them—had this profound of an effect on him.

The sea breeze swept past them, sending the long wavy strands of Sage's hair fluttering. A few pieces clung to her cheek. It was instinct for him to reach out and swipe the strands off to the side. But as his finger made contact with her smooth skin, it was like a switch had been turned on inside of him. His bottled-up attraction was released and his only thought was how soon they could be alone.

Trey struggled to fight off his pent-up longings. He was a sworn bachelor. He shouldn't care if things didn't work out with Sage. In any other scenario, he would have cut things off by now and moved on. But he couldn't walk away from her.

And if he stood here much longer, he might give in to his desire to pull her into his arms and taste her sweet kisses again and again. It was as though gravity was drawing their bodies closer together.

As though Sage could sense the direction of his

thoughts, she took a step back. "The movie screening should be starting soon. It's almost dark."

Disappointment assailed him. "It is." Glancing down, he noticed his empty glass. "And I could use another cold drink. How about you?"

"I'm good. Thanks." She placed the straw between her glossy lips and sucked.

Watching her do such a simple act got to him. It conjured up other more heated thoughts. He needed to walk away and clear his head. He needed more than a cold drink—he needed a cold shower or a dip in the Mediterranean. Although, he didn't think their superstar host would appreciate him diving off the edge of the yacht in the middle of a party. But then again, it would make this party the highlight of the festival.

Trey was in no hurry to get his drink. It was just as well as there was quite a crowd at the bar. This time he requested ice water. Maybe it would cool him down.

With his icy drink in hand, he moved off to the side. When he glanced back to where he'd left Sage, the spot was empty. His gaze scanned the area and then he spotted her dancing with some man that he'd never seen before.

The man was holding her awfully close and the look on her face wasn't a happy one. Trey set aside his unfinished drink and moved toward the dance floor. He paused at the side, not sure how Sage would feel about him storming in and dragging her away from this man. But that's exactly what he wanted to do.

When her gaze caught his, she mouthed, *Help me.*

That was all the encouragement he needed. He wove his way past the other couples and stepped up to Sage. "Excuse me. Can I cut in?"

Before the man could say anything, Sage said, "Yes. I do owe you a dance."

The man frowned at both of them before he relinquished his hold on Sage and stormed off. Trey took her in his arms. He loved the way her slight form felt next to him. When her head leaned close to his, he got a whiff of her jasmine scent. He breathed in deeper.

"You know," he said, "the last time we danced together, it didn't go so well."

"That was your fault. You rejected my kiss."

"I didn't reject you. I would never reject you."

Sage pulled back to look into his eyes. "Then what would you call it?"

"I didn't want things to get complicated. Not before I told you my true identity."

She blinked. "That's why you pulled away?"

"It's the honest truth."

He could sense something shifting within her. As they continued to dance, it was like she was digesting this bit of news and figuring out where it left them. He wanted to ask, but he decided not to push his luck.

Tomorrow was her birthday and he had a couple of surprises planned for her. Hopefully it'd be enough to finish tearing down the wall between them. For now, holding her close would have to be enough.

CHAPTER SIXTEEN

THE EVENING WAS still a mystery.

Sage had the French doors leading to her private balcony open, letting in the sea breeze. Below her room was the pool and gardens, but tonight there were white tents scattered about lit up with torches. It appeared Trey was throwing her a birthday dinner.

She had to admit she was anxious to find out what he had planned. She was quickly learning he had a flair for the dramatic. But then again, she wouldn't be opposed to a private candlelit dinner.

Her heart thump-thumped at the memory of how Trey had held her close on the yacht. He'd have kissed her, if she'd let him. So why hadn't she?

As upset as she had been with the way he entered her life, she now knew he hadn't set out to hurt anyone, except maybe himself…and his father. But Trey had changed. He was beginning to see that family and legacies meant something—they meant a lot.

She wanted to believe they could make a new start. Ever since he'd bought her the stunning pendant, the walls around her heart had started to fall. His encouragement, unwavering support and constant attention had shown her that she wasn't wrong about Trey. He was an amazing man.

Sage put the final touches on her hair that she'd swept up and back with one smooth curl trailing down her back. She quickly put on the dangly earrings she'd borrowed from her roommate. She stepped back from the mirror to get an overall look at her appearance.

It was a sexy, daring fluff of violet material otherwise known as an amazing dress. She turned in a circle in front of the mirror. The organza fabric practically floated around her.

She felt like one of those stars that walked the red carpet. This dress wasn't an ordinary dress. It was from a big-name designer who she always watched on the award shows to check out his latest designs. Little did she know that one day she'd be wearing one.

And then there were the heels. They made her heart pitter-patter every time she looked at them. They were a deep purple satin with a closed toe. Small crystals bordered the opening. A thin strap wrapped around her ankle.

Earlier today, Trey had escorted her to the boutiques in town. He insisted on getting her a birthday gift. She'd tried on almost every dress in her size. She'd also tried on matching shoes because the saleslady insisted. And, well, what woman could pass up wearing the most stunning pair of heels.

In the end, Sage insisted the dress was more than enough of a birthday gift. The shoes were just too much. But when she'd returned to the château, she'd found the boutique had delivered not only the dress but also the shoes. Trey obviously had selective hearing. She should insist they be returned, but shoes were her weakness. Did that make her a bad person?

A knock at her door had her rushing over to answer it. She pulled it open, ready to thank Trey for his tremendous generosity. However, when she took in his still-damp hair styled to perfection and his black tux, the words stuck in her throat. This man could definitely wear a suit with his broad shoulders, muscled chest and slim waist. Oh, yes, he looked like a star.

"You are breathtaking." Trey's voice jarred her from her thoughts.

"Thank you. I was just thinking the same about you."

"What?" He acted all innocent. "You mean this old thing?"

She laughed. "That old thing looks like a million dollars on you."

A sexy smile lit up his tan face and made his eyes twinkle. When he looked at her that way, her heart raced. He made her feel like she was the only woman in the world for him. "Why, thank you, ma'am." He held out his arm to her. "Shall we?"

She glanced back in the room, feeling as though she'd forgotten something. And then she realized what it was, her press badge and the pendant. She'd been wearing both for so many days that it felt strange not to have them on this evening.

She turned back to Trey. "Yes." As they were nearing the top of the steps, she said, "You really went out of your way. But you shouldn't have—"

"Yes, I should. I love to make you smile."

She stared deep into his eyes. "All you have to do is be with me to make me smile."

"I feel the same way." He moved his free hand until it was covering the hand she had tucked in the crook of his arm. He stared deep into her eyes. "This evening is for you. Now let's get the princess to the ball."

He wasn't serious? Was he?

"Trey, what have you done? You didn't actually plan a ball, did you?"

His face beamed. "Just a little something to say happy birthday."

"Thank you for this memorable day, these fabulous clothes and shoes. You're like my fairy godmother."

He shook his head. "I'd rather be your prince. I'm not much into wearing the tiara and dress thing."

She laughed. "Whatever you want to call yourself, I think you're wonderful."

"I think the same thing about you, too." He released her hand from his arm. "Now get going."

"But aren't you coming, too?"

"I'll be right behind you. But the belle of the ball needs to make her big entrance."

That meant there were people downstairs. She glanced down at the landing, but she didn't see anyone. Perhaps they were waiting out on the patio.

"Trey, tell me what you've done."

"You'll have to go see for yourself."

Her heart raced in that nervous, giddy sort of way. It tickled the back of her throat. And she struggled to suppress a nervous giggle. For so long now, she felt as though she'd had the weight of the world upon her shoulders. But this magical trip to France had her feeling so much lighter—so much more optimistic about the future.

Maybe it was all just a rosy illusion. Maybe she had too much sun and bubbly. Or maybe it was having Trey in her life. Either way, she couldn't be happier.

She held on to the rail as she made her way down the steps. She wasn't so sure she trusted her knees to hold her up. And with the other hand, she clutched the long skirt of her designer gown. She almost expected flashes to go off, like they had at the red-carpet movie premieres. Not that she was anyone special. She was a nobody, living a fairy tale.

Two steps from the landing, she stopped and

glanced over her shoulder. Trey was still standing at the top, where she'd left him. He gestured for her to head into the living room.

She turned to find the double doors leading to the living room closed. They were never closed. So her surprise must lie within. Her heart leaped into her throat.

Willing her legs to cooperate, she successfully stepped onto the marble floor of the grand foyer. She started for the living room when the doors swung open and a bunch of smiling faces appeared.

"Surprise!" The house echoed with their happy voices.

A smile immediately pulled at Sage's lips. He'd planned a surprise party for her. She was so touched. No one had done anything like this since…since her father was alive. Her vision started to blur with tears of joy. She quickly blinked them away and thanked everyone.

The next thing she knew Trey was by her side. She turned to him. "You threw me a surprise party?"

He nodded, looking a little worried. "You like it, don't you?"

She sent him a huge, ear-to-ear smile. "I love it. Thank you."

His heart swelled with a warm sensation.

Trey brushed aside the unfamiliar feeling. There

was no time to analyze it now. At this moment, his full focus had to be on making Sage happy. That was the entire point of this evening.

If it was at all in his power, he would do whatever it took to make it up to Sage for his deception. Decisions have consequences. He thought he knew that—he thought he understood—but then he'd made a big decision and the consequences turned out not to be his alone to shoulder. He wondered if his father ever came to the same conclusion.

Trey halted his thoughts. Their two scenarios were not the same. His father walked away from his family for a business. Trey hadn't walked away from Sage. He wanted to think that somehow they could start over. Was that even possible?

He turned to her. His gaze lingered, taking in the dazzling sparkle of her eyes and the smile on her beautiful face. In that moment, he was filled with the notion that anything was possible if you wanted it bad enough. And he wanted Sage to be happy—with the night and with him. He wanted to be close to her again. He wanted her to bestow her sunny smile on him. He wanted all of her. Period.

And tonight was his chance to dazzle her, spoil her and just plain make her happy. So far it appeared to be working. Just wait until she found out what else he'd planned, including a very special present.

He cleared his throat. "I remembered what you

told me about your father taking you on a trip for your birthday and I wanted to do something to honor that."

"Trey, what did you do?"

A hush fell over the crowd as all eyes were on them.

"Don't go getting too excited. I know we have to remain here in Cannes until the end of the festival and then return to California for the board meeting, so I thought I'd bring some of the world here to you." He took her by the hand. The crowd parted, clearing a path for them into the dining room. It had been cleared of furniture and replaced with a very long buffet with a white linen tablecloth. "Here you'll find cuisine flown in from around the world."

Her mouth gaped. Her gaze moved from him to the food and then back to him. "You really flew all of this in for me?"

"I did."

"No one has ever done anything so thoughtful for me." And then her eyes shimmered with tears.

Panic clutched Trey. Tears weren't good. Tears were out of his realm of control. They made him uncomfortable.

"I… I can make it all go away," he said out of desperation.

She blinked the tears away. "Go away? Never. I love it." She leaned forward and gave him a hug. It was brief, but it was a bridge that he hoped to build upon. "I'm sure all of your guests are hungry. I know I am."

"But you don't look happy. And this is your birthday. You should have whatever makes you happy."

"Okay, then..." She hesitated as though considering what would make her happiest. "For tonight, I want to pretend that all of that nastiness with Elsa and the thing with you never happened. I want to pretend the magazine isn't in jeopardy and, for the first time since my parents died, all is right in the world."

That was a really steep wish, but she was the birthday girl. "Tonight you will be a princess. And your wish is my command." He bowed and waved toward the table.

A smile bloomed on her face. She walked over to the table. He joined her and explained the menu. *Pho* and *goi cuon*—noodle soup and spring rolls from Vietnam. Moussaka and baklava from Greece. Polenta and meatballs from Italy. And the list went on, with treats from the Philippines, Japan, India, Spain and more.

Sage turned to him. "I could never eat all of this. But I'm going to give it my best effort."

He laughed. "That's a plan."

Once she filled her plate to the point of having absolutely no room left, she turned. There was no one behind them. She glanced to the crowd of finely dressed guests.

"Please, everyone, eat. Don't let this culinary miracle go to waste."

Everyone smiled and wished her happy birthday. Then they all got in line.

Trey led her out to the torch-lit balcony where linen-covered tables awaited them. The centerpieces were hurricane lamps that created a warm glow. He pulled out her chair and then he took the seat next to her.

"Thank you for this. It's amazing." She took a bite of the tiramisu from Italy.

"You don't have to keep thanking me. I wanted to do it."

"Really?" Her gaze searched his. "Or were you just trying to appease me?"

"There's nothing to appease. Remember? You wished away our past?"

Her eyes widened. "So I did."

"I really did enjoy doing this for you. It was a challenge finding all of the restaurants that were willing to ship food via air. It takes home delivery to a whole new level."

"It does. But..." She took another bite of tiramisu. "Mmm...it was so worth it."

"I'm glad you approve."

"Approve? I'm floored. This is the best birthday present ever."

"You misunderstand. This isn't your present."

"It's not?" She sent him a puzzled look.

"No. This is just your party. I have something special for your gift."

"I don't know how you could plan anything more special than this. You've already done too much."

"Seeing you smile made it worth it."

And then they set to work savoring all the delicacies. Trey couldn't take his eyes off Sage. She practically glowed with happiness.

Tonight there were no worries about his father or the magazine or trying to be someone he wasn't. Tonight he was Trey, Sage's escort. And his only concern was to keep that smile on her face for as long as possible.

Sage pushed away her plate. "I am stuffed."

"Then we'll have to dance off some of those calories."

"Dance?" Her eyes opened wide. "I don't think I can move. The seams on my dress might split."

"I highly doubt it. You didn't eat that much. And you have to make room for these." Just then Maria arrived with a platter of cookies. "These were flown in from LA."

Sage gave the tray a once-over and then her mouth lifted into a big smile. "Are those Louise's double chocolate cookies?"

He nodded. "She wanted to do something special for your birthday."

"I love those cookies." She reached out for one.

"I thought you were stuffed."

A guilty smile lit up her face. "I have a little room left."

"Don't worry. Maria will make sure you have plenty of leftovers."

"Happy birthday, ma'am." Maria left her a couple of cookies and then took the tray away.

Sage's gaze met his. "Tonight is like a dream."

"Enough of sitting out here. It's time to go join your party." He got to his feet and held his hand out to her. "And I think it's time for your present."

She placed her hand in his and got to her feet. She stood mere inches from him and lifted her chin until their gazes met. "Whatever it is, take it back. I just can't accept anything else. This is a night that I will never, ever forget."

In that moment, he was tempted to pull her closer. He ached to feel her soft curves nestled against him. He longed to taste her sweet lips again. If only he hadn't messed things up.

Still, her entire mood tonight was so different— so relaxed. Would she let him kiss her? Or would she shove him aside?

The truth was he couldn't take the risk. This was Sage's night. He wouldn't do anything to ruin it. He'd just have to push aside his desires and focus on keeping Sage happy. That was the important part.

"Trey?" Her voice was soft, like it was floating on the gentle sea breeze brushing their skin.

He took a step back as he gave himself a mental shake. "I can't take back your present."

"Did you go and get it personalized?"

"Not exactly. But it was definitely chosen just for you."

"Okay. You have me curious now. What did you get me?"

"Come this way." He presented his arm to her.

She gave him a leery look as she complied. They walked into the house. He was suddenly having second thoughts about his surprise. Sage had said that she wanted to forget about the magazine—about the looming deadline with the *QTR* board. And his gift for her would be a reminder of all that.

But it was too late now. He already had all the wheels in motion. He could only hope she would like it.

"Ladies and gentlemen." He waited a moment for silence to descend over the room. "Thank you all for coming. I hope you've gotten plenty to eat. If not, we have lots of extras. This evening is just getting started. There will be dancing in the other room and the bar is open. And it's now time for the birthday girl to find out about her gift."

Trey turned to Sage.

"All these wonderful people are friends and neighbors. They've come here tonight not only to wish you a happy birthday but also to present you with a gift."

Sage stood there looking as though she was not quite sure what to make of what he was saying. He liked being able to leave her speechless. Perhaps he'd have to work on doing it more often.

"These friends are all renowned in their fields. Some are in entertainment. Some are in fundraising. Others are in research or fashion. They have a great many talents. Some live in Europe year-round. Others split their time between here and the States. And they've all agreed to give you an interview and heads-up for their upcoming social engagements."

Sage's mouth gaped as her gaze moved around the congested room. And then realizing that her mouth was hanging open, she forced her lips together. "Thank you all. I don't know what to say. I am stunned and so grateful to all of you for making this the most amazing night of my life."

Trey smiled. And the night was only getting started. He was looking forward to holding her in his arms and guiding her around the dance floor.

CHAPTER SEVENTEEN

THIS HAD TO be a dream.

There was no way the evening had been real. Now that the guests were gone and the lights had been dimmed, Sage knew she should go to sleep, but she was too wound up.

The pieces needed to create a path to her future had fallen into place. Thanks to Trey. Those guests hadn't just been random people. They were all remarkable, from actors to athletes to prizewinning authors to world movers and shakers. They all had diverse and intriguing stories to tell. And she planned to give their voices a platform from which the world could hear them.

"Come dance with me," Trey coaxed.

"But we can't. There isn't even any music."

"We don't need music." Trey took her in his arms.

Their bodies swayed together as though they were made for each other. Sage's cheeks grew sore from smiling so much. She didn't know it was possible to be this happy.

"This the most perfect birthday. Thank you."

"I'm glad you enjoyed it."

"Enjoyed it doesn't even come close to describing how I feel right now."

A waiter went to pass them with a tray full of dishes. Trey stopped him and asked for two glasses of bubbly. They resumed dancing while the waiter sought out the requested bubbly.

Sage slipped off her heels and moved across the floor in her bare feet. Trey twirled her around and dipped her. It was like a scene right out of a black and white movie where she was the leading lady. Best of all, Trey was the leading man.

The waiter came to a stop next to them with a tray of bubbly. Trey took two flutes and handed her one.

He gazed into her eyes. "Here's to the most beautiful birthday girl."

"And here's to the perfect date."

They clinked their glasses together and then sipped at the champagne that tickled Sage's nose. He took the glass from her hand and set it aside. He took her back in his arms and stared deeply into her eyes. "I wish I could make you smile like this all of the time."

"Who says you can't?" She was flirting with him. It was dangerous but she couldn't stop herself.

A smile lifted his very tempting lips. "And what would I have to do to make you smile all of the time?"

Maybe it was the bubbly or the exhaustion as it was now the wee hours of the morning, but she felt a bit daring. She lifted up on her tiptoes and leaned into him.

She whispered, "This would keep me smiling."

She pressed her lips to his. He didn't move. He stood perfectly still. She wasn't even sure that he was breathing.

Oh, no. Had she read too much into the evening? What if he rejected her? She hadn't thought this through. Panic consumed her and she froze.

And then his lips moved over hers. His touch was gentle yet stirring. Her heart thump-thumped. He gripped her waist, pulling her snug against his firm chest.

She wanted to see where this kiss would lead them, but there were still questions—nagging questions. How could she trust him when there was still so much left unsaid between them?

The conflicting emotions within her tempered her desires. They had to talk first. The good stuff was going to have to wait. The last time she'd totally trusted a man, he'd lied to her. She couldn't have that happen again—not when she cared so much for Trey.

It took all her effort to brace her hands against his muscled chest and push. Her gaze immediately met the unspoken questions reflected in Trey's eyes.

"We need to talk," she said above the sound of her pounding heart. And then realizing that her hands were still on him, she lowered them to her sides.

"Maybe it can wait till later. I had something else in mind for now." He sent her a playful smile.

"This is serious." She couldn't let herself get sidetracked. She didn't want to have regrets later.

The smile disappeared from his face. "What do you want to talk about?"

"You."

His brows rose. "Okay. What do you want to know?"

"I want to know if there are any more secrets."

"No, there aren't." He stared deep into her eyes. "I never meant to hurt you. When I first thought up the idea of going undercover, I didn't take into consideration all the people I would have to lie to. I deeply regret it."

"But why didn't you tell me later on? When things started to change between us?" She really needed to know—to understand.

"I meant to but it never seemed like the right time." He raked his fingers through his hair. "I... I was afraid you would hate me."

"Were you going to let the lie just go on and on?"

He shook his head. "I'd planned to tell you, the same day that we ran into Elsa."

"And she ruined your plans?"

He nodded as he reached out, taking her hands

in his own. "If I could go back and do things different, I would. I swear."

There was something different about Trey tonight. He was—she stared at him—he was filled with remorse. The weight of what he'd done showed in the lines now etching his handsome face. Lying to her—to everyone at the magazine—hadn't come easy and it had cost him. That knowledge brought her comfort.

But she'd also witnessed a different side of him while in Cannes. He was a team player and he was willing to put himself out there to make her happy. And he'd changed his mind about his legacy.

She could understand how hurt he'd been after his parents split up. Losing a close family dynamic is traumatic and then for Trey to think his father hadn't cared about him would have colored the way he'd looked at the world.

"Do you promise to be honest with me from now on?"

This was the deal breaker. She couldn't have someone in her life that she couldn't trust.

He stared straight into her eyes and, without blinking, he said, "I do. I swear it."

"That is the best birthday gift." She leaned in and kissed him.

This time he was the one to pull away. He turned and flipped off the lights. "Let's go upstairs."

He held his hand out to her and she placed her

hand in his. Together, they ascended the staircase. Quietly they made their way down the hallway.

Outside her bedroom, he kissed her lightly on the lips. "Happy birthday."

When he turned to walk away, she said, "Don't go."

Trey hesitated. "It's late. And—"

"Don't go."

He reached out. His thumb gently stroked her cheek. "I want you to be sure about this—about me."

"I am. You made a mistake and you've tried to make amends. I forgive you."

"You do?"

She smiled and nodded. "It's in the past. This is a new beginning for us."

Sage opened the bedroom door and led him by the hand inside. Trey closed the door behind him. And then he was holding her in his arms.

"Are you sure about this?" he asked.

"I'm sure about you and me. It's going to be a perfect night."

Sage lifted up on her tiptoes and pressed her lips to his. This time there was no hesitation—no butterfly kisses. In the darkness, there was hunger and desire.

Her heart pounded so loud that she could no longer hear anything else. The only thing she knew was that she was no longer alone. Trey had filled in the cracks in her heart.

And tomorrow—

She cut off that thought as she fell back against the bed. With his lips teasing hers, there was no room for thoughts of tomorrow. There was only the here and now. And Trey. That was enough.

CHAPTER EIGHTEEN

EVEN BEFORE HER eyes were open, Sage had a smile on her face.

This was going to be the most wonderful day. How could it not be after such an amazing night? From the birthday party that topped all parties to Trey's heartfelt apology to winding up in his arms all night long.

Her hand ran over the sheets and found the spot next to her empty and cold.

Sage's eyes fluttered open. She scanned the room, finding herself all alone. She wasn't sure what to make of it. Was Trey just anxious to get on with his day? Or did he regret their evening together?

She rushed through her shower and dressed. She was just putting on her makeup when the door swung open. There stood Trey with a tray of food in his arms.

"Hey, sleepyhead, I thought you'd still be in bed after being up most of the night." He smiled at her.

At last, she could take an easy breath. Everything was going to be all right. They were going to be all right. She smiled back.

"I couldn't sleep the day away. Tomorrow is the end of the festival."

"And you want to get out there and line up more potential interviews?"

"Actually, thanks to you, the magazine's calendar is filled. So I thought I would take these last two days to soak up the atmosphere and just relax. We could have a perfectly relaxing afternoon together."

"That sounds very tempting, but I'm going to have to take a pass. I hope you have a good time."

"Wait. What? Why aren't you coming with me?" She was hoping they'd spend the day together.

"Because while we've been concentrating on lining up star-studded interviews, the work back at the office has been piling up. And I need to get to it."

"Oh." Disappointment welled up in her. "You mean your software business."

"That, too. But I was referring to the magazine. Remember, as far as everyone knows, I'm still your assistant."

"But you aren't. You don't have to do that stuff. I can handle it."

"What you can do is walk this way." He led her out to her own private balcony. He placed the food on the table and then turned to her. "Now, sit and eat. And then go have fun."

"But without you?"

"I promise I'll work as fast as I can and then catch up with you."

"I could stay and help. We'd get it done twice as fast."

He shook his head. "I've got this. But if you'd like, I could have Louise start lining up applicants for you to interview when you get back to California."

"But won't she find that strange, considering she doesn't know who you really are?"

He lowered his gaze. "I was going to tell her. I figured that way by the time we get back to LA everyone in the office would know the truth."

It would be best coming from him. "Go ahead and tell her. But I don't know about lining up applicants. With the board meeting coming up, it might be a pointless endeavor."

"Stop worrying. With all the progress you've made, there's no way they'll shut down the magazine. It's going to be the crown jewel of QTR International." He leaned forward and gave her a quick kiss like it was something they did every morning.

And then he was gone. She sighed. She knew he was still trying to set things right between them and that just made her—what? The feeling was just bubbling beneath the surface. It was a word that she'd never used in connection with anyone—until now.

She loved Trey.

She smiled—truly smiled. She couldn't remember the last time she smiled this much. And it was thanks to him.

Now it was her turn to do something special for

him. And she knew exactly what it would be. She grabbed her cell phone and scrolled down until she found the number for Quentin senior. Her finger hesitated over the send button. If Trey had been able to learn to appreciate his family's magazine, maybe there was hope for him to forgive his father.

She pressed Send. The phone started to ring.

This was a chance for all of them to have a fresh start.

It was the final evening of the festival.

They were invited to the swankiest gala and Trey was anxious to escort Sage. Tonight would be their grand swan song. He knew when they returned to California that they'd have to contend with their jobs. His would take him back to San Francisco while her position kept her in LA.

Sure, they'd stay in close contact at first. There'd be phone calls every day and weekends together. But he knew from past experience that the phone calls would slowly trickle off and the weekend get-aways would grow farther and farther apart.

It wasn't what he wanted, but it was all he had to offer her. But for tonight, they could pretend their future together was rosy. Because try as he might, he'd come to care for Sage more than he'd ever cared for anyone. And he didn't know what to do with all these new feelings.

He straightened the tie to his tux, buttoned his

jacket and then headed for the bedroom door. It was time to pick up his date. He couldn't wait to see what she was wearing this evening. Between the gowns he'd gotten for her and what she'd packed in all those suitcases, he didn't think she'd worn the same outfit twice since they'd arrived in Cannes.

He rapped his knuckles on her bedroom door. "Come in."

He opened the door to find Sage in a long, slinky silver dress. She was standing with her bare back to him. It was quite a tempting sight. And then there was the way the dress hugged her hips. It was perfect on her.

She turned to him. "You're just in time."

"I am?" He swallowed hard as he took in the front of the dress with its dipping neckline. The back was good but the front was amazing. "I mean, I am. You are a knockout."

She smiled but the smile didn't quite reach her eyes. "Thank you. Are you sure this dress works? I could change into something else." She moved to the wardrobe and swung open the doors. "What color would you like to see me in?"

"Slow down. That dress really suits you. Every guy at the gala will want to dance with you." He walked up to her and pulled her into his arms. "But you'll have to let them know that your dance card is full."

"It is?"

He nodded. "Yes, it is. I intend to spend the evening with you in my arms."

He leaned forward and kissed her. Her lips were so soft and so willing. It would be so easy to just skip the event and stay in for the evening. In fact, the idea quite appealed to him.

But then Sage pulled back. "We can't be late."

"Sure we can." He tried to pull her back to him but she was too fast for him.

She moved to the dresser and picked up a necklace. She held it out to him. "I can't seem to get this on. Could you do it for me?"

"Sure." When he went to take it from her, he noticed a slight tremor in her hands. "Is something wrong?"

She glanced away. "No."

He put the necklace on her and then, putting his hand on her shoulder, propelled her around to face him. "I know there's something wrong."

"Why would something be wrong? It's going to be a perfect night as I'm with the perfect man."

"You're jumpy and not acting like yourself. What's the matter?"

"Nothing." She said it too quickly and avoided his gaze.

"Sage—"

Chime. Chime.

He turned to the hallway and then back to her. "I wonder who that could be."

She turned to the mirror and put on her earrings. "Why don't you go see? I'll be right there as soon as I grab my heels."

There was an uneasy feeling churning in the pit of his stomach. He had that feeling before, right before a hacker had decimated his software prototype. He shook off the feeling. He assured himself that nothing was going to go wrong tonight. The worst was behind them. Sage knew the truth about him.

And she was probably just nervous about getting all dressed up and mingling with the rich and famous. It could be a lot of pressure, trying to figure out what to say and how to act.

He assured himself that he was reading too much into Sage's actions as he walked down the steps. Maria had already answered the door. He could hear her speaking, but he couldn't make out the other voice.

When he reached the bottom step, he paused. There was no one in the foyer. Maria must have showed their guest into the living room.

Maria exited the room and nearly ran into him. Her face was white like she'd seen a ghost. "*Monsieur*, I was coming to get you. I wasn't sure what to do. I hope I didn't do the wrong thing."

"Calm down, Maria. Did someone hurt you?"

She shook her head but her eyes were filled with worry. "It's you I'm worried about."

"Me? But I'm fine." And then he realized she was referring to the presence of their guest. "I've got this. You can go."

"Are...are you sure?"

That uneasy feeling in his gut was now much more like a knot. "I'm sure."

He turned to the doorway. He had a feeling he knew who was waiting for him, but he longed to be wrong. He would give anything for it to be someone else.

His feet felt as though they'd been cast in concrete. A steel band felt as though it was cinched around his chest, growing ever tighter. With determined effort, he put one foot in front of the other. And when he stepped into the entrance to the living room, his worst fears were confirmed.

A man stood facing the fireplace as though looking at the framed family photos. Apparently he hadn't heard Trey's arrival. That was fine with Trey. He needed a moment to figure out what to say to this unwanted visitor.

The man was about his height. He appeared to still have all of his hair, although it was silver now.

There was nothing outwardly striking about the man. Nothing to let on how mean he could really be. Any other person would probably think that he was a nice old man. They wouldn't know the damage he'd caused or the life he'd destroyed.

And Trey knew why he was here. This was

Sage's doing. This was why she'd been so nervous upstairs. She knew he didn't want this man in his house—in his life. And yet she'd brought him here anyway.

"You are not welcome." Trey's voice came firm and steady, even though he didn't feel like it on the inside.

His father turned. He didn't say a word at first. It was as though his father was taking in his appearance and sizing him up. "I can see some of your mother in you. That steely determination written all over your face is just like her."

"You have no right to talk about my mother. You lost that right a long time ago."

His father nodded and said in an even tone, "I understand."

Trey couldn't take his father's ambivalence. He wanted his father to be as worked up as he was. He wanted his father to show some sort of emotion.

"What are you doing here?"

"I came to see you. I thought it was past time."

Trey vehemently shook his head. It was never a good time for this man to intrude in his life. "I told you at my mother's funeral that I never wanted to see you again. Why would you think that has changed?"

"I asked him to come." Sage's voice came from behind him.

Trey turned. "You shouldn't have done it. You

are meddling in something that you don't understand."

Her eyes pleaded with him to understand. "You only get one go-around in this life. When it's over, you don't get any do-overs. No second chances. Don't miss an opportunity to get back your family."

Trey shook his head. "Sage, you can't make this into the happy family you so desperately want."

"Don't be mad at her, son. She was only doing what she thought was best for you."

He swung back around to face his father. "I'm not your son. You gave up that privilege a long time ago."

Trey turned and started to walk away when Sage reached out and caught his arm with her hand. "Please, just hear him out and then you can go."

"I can't. He has nothing I want to hear. He had almost thirty years to say it. Now it's too late."

His father's voice filled with emotion. "I did try to say it, but your mother…she refused to let me see you."

Trey swung around. "That's a lie. She never would have turned you away. She told me how you wouldn't even take her phone calls."

"You only heard her side of the story. But I have one, too. I came back for you, but she wouldn't let me inside. She said you were at school. Another time she said you were at a friend's house. She always had an excuse to keep us apart. We argued. It seemed like that's all we ever did in the end. And then she threatened to take you away so that I would never find you."

"I don't believe you."

"She did it. She took you and it took me almost a year to find you. You must have been about six at the time. She moved to Paris and stayed in a small apartment."

Trey was about to deny it but then the memories started to come back to him. He'd hated the tiny apartment. It was nothing like the château. It stunk and he wasn't allowed outside to play. He'd missed his bedroom, his friends and, most of all, Maria.

"See, you do remember the move. Your mother wanted to punish me. And her greatest weapon was keeping you from me." His father's eyes grew shiny with unshed tears. And his voice grew gruff. "When I found the apartment, we had a terrible row. The police were called. In the end, I agreed to keep my distance if she would take you back to the château where I knew there would be people around to see to your safety."

Trey remembered awaking to a ruckus. His mother had told him it was a problem with the neighbors. He had no reason not to believe her at the time. But his father's words were starting to answer some questions.

Was it possible his father wasn't the villain that

his mother had painted? Trey's head started to pound. It was just too much.

"I can't do this." Trey turned and walked out of the room.

Sage followed him to the front steps. "Trey, don't go. I'm sorry I invited your father here. I shouldn't have done it. Let's just forget this happened and go to the gala. It'll be the perfect end—"

"Stop." He just couldn't take any more of her looking at him like he was the answer to her dreams. "Ever since the birthday party, you keep saying that everything is perfect now. It's not. I'm not."

"I know you're upset, but we'll get through this together. That's what couples do. They work through the thick and thin."

He shook his head. "We're not a couple."

Her mouth gaped as though his words had stabbed her. He hated to see the pain reflected in her eyes, but it was time to bring her back down to earth before she got in any deeper.

"Sage, I do care about you, how could I not? You are sweet, kind and thoughtful. You would make any man the perfect wife, but not me. I don't fit into your plan for a perfect family."

"That's not true."

"Isn't it? Didn't you bring my father here in order to bring us back together? You want that perfect family that was stolen from you. And you deserve the perfect life. But I can't be part of that perfect picture."

A tear slipped down her cheek. "You can if you want to be."

He shook his head. "I am broken. You just heard me with my father. With those two as my role models, I'd have no chance of making the perfect husband or father. I'm too damaged on the inside. I would never make you happy. You are better off without me."

It took every bit of willpower to turn his back on her and walk away.

"But you do make me happy." The whisper of her voice was carried by the breeze.

He assured himself that he was doing what was best for her.

But it sure didn't feel like it.

CHAPTER NINETEEN

THE TRIP TO the French Riviera had been a complete and utter disaster.

And she had no one to blame but herself.

Sage had been back in Los Angeles for a week now and she hadn't heard one word from Trey. Every time she walked past his empty desk, it was like a nail was being driven into her heart. Sharp and painful.

Today was the board meeting. With Trey being the acting CEO, there was no way he could avoid being in the same room with her. She'd arrived at the meeting with a comprehensive report that she'd worked all week to finalize. It detailed where the magazine had been financially and circulation-wise when she took over. It showed the increase in supermarkets and bookstores that were willing to carry the revamped format as well as their online subscriptions. And then there was the calendar of extraordinary individuals as well as global events that they would be featuring for not one but two years. That last part was mainly thanks to Trey and she felt bad about not being able to thank him.

As soon as the meeting had concluded, Trey stood. The breath caught in her throat as she waited for him to approach her. Instead he turned and left the room without a word to her. Other board members stopped to speak with her. Some had questions about a portion of the presentation and others wanted to compliment her on the work she'd done so far.

Why had she ever thought that bringing Trey face-to-face with his father was a good idea? She knew that Trey had been terribly hurt in the past. She had just hoped that somehow father and son could find a new start—something she would never have with either of her parents.

As she made her way back to her office, she couldn't help but think about Trey's parting words to her: *"I don't fit into your plan for a perfect family."* Was he right? Was she looking for the "perfect" family to make up for the one she'd lost?

She'd never really thought about it. Not until now. There had never been an opportunity for her to consider having a family of her own. Sure, there had been Charlie, but their relationship hadn't escalated to the point of thinking about marriage or a family. At least she could be thankful for that one small saving grace. Because she'd made a total fool of herself by believing all of his lies.

But Trey was nothing like Charlie. And then she thought about how they'd met. Trey had lied to her about who he was and what he wanted. But he'd done everything in his power to make it up to her—to show her that he wasn't that person, that he was better.

And the thing was she really liked the real Trey. She liked him so much that she'd wanted him to have the one thing she couldn't have—a family. She'd been so sure if Trey could open his heart and listen to his father that they could find their way back to each other. And it had been a disaster.

Now, not only was Trey out of her life, but soon Happy would be gone, too. She'd thought about stopping by Louise's office because she was still puppy-sitting Happy. She could really use some puppy kisses and snuggles. Not that he was hers, but in the time they'd spent together, he'd snuck into her heart. But she resisted the temptation. She had to get used to life without Trey or Happy in it.

She walked into her office and came to a stop. There was Happy with his tail wagging. Her heavy heart felt a little lighter and her downturned lips lifted into a genuine smile.

"Hey there, buddy." She set her belongings on the end of the couch and knelt down.

Happy rushed up to her and lathered her with kisses. She scooped him up in her arms and gave him a hug. She didn't understand what he was doing here, but she was so happy to see him.

"Oh, there you are." Louise's voice came from the doorway.

Sage turned. "Were you looking for me? Or the dog?"

"I didn't know if you'd return after the board meeting. How did it go?"

"It's a closed vote. And it might come down to Trey's vote."

"But I thought you said he was on board with the magazine now."

"That was before."

"Before what?"

"Before I decided to play God with his life."

"Oops. That doesn't sound good." An indecisive look settled on her face. "This sounds like it's going to need some coffee and a Danish or two."

Sage moved to her desk chair, knowing that as the boss she should insist they get to work, but her heart just wasn't in it today. Maybe if she talked to Louise, it'd help clear her head. But something told her neither the talking nor the baked goods would help the ache in her heart.

Louise hurried back into the office balancing a plate of goodies and two coffees. She placed everything on the desk and then took a seat as though settling in for the whole sordid story.

Sage didn't want to get into the painful details, but maybe someone else's perspective would help. She needed someone to tell her that what she'd done hadn't been as awful as it felt—even if it hadn't ended the way she'd been hoping.

And so the words came out slowly at first. The more she talked about her time with Trey, the more she missed him. And then as she spoke, she started to see things differently. She finally understood what Trey had been trying to tell her—she was trying to make him do, feel and say what she wanted.

"I can't believe I didn't see this sooner," Sage said more to herself than Louise.

"Sometimes when you're so intimately involved in a situation, it's hard to see things clearly."

Tears rushed to her eyes. "But I hurt not only Trey but his father, too." She blinked away the tears. "I made things so much worse for both of them. And that's not what I meant to do."

"But you brought them back together. That's more than anyone has done in years."

"That's not a good thing. You didn't witness the tension and the anger that filled the room."

"Did they speak to each other?"

Sage nodded. "But none of it was constructive."

Louise's eyes filled with sympathy. "You did it out of the goodness of your heart."

Happy rounded the desk and put his paws up on Sage's lap. She picked him up and gave him another hug. "Do you think Trey has discarded Happy because of me?"

Louise shook her head. "I talked to him last night. He said he had a few things to take care of and then he offered to pay me for puppy-sitting.

Like I would take money for watching that furry ball of love." A big smile filled her face as her gaze landed on Happy. "You and I, we're buddies, aren't we?"

Arf!

A smile tugged at Sage's lips. "If he changes his mind, I'll take him."

"You'll have to stand in line. This little guy already stole my heart."

"I'm sure Trey is missing you." She couldn't resist giving Happy another hug and recalling the way they'd worked together to help Happy. That's when she'd let her guard down long enough to see that there was so much more to Trey than his good looks.

"I'm guessing after everything you told me that Trey won't be coming to the office anymore." Louise's voice roused Sage from her thoughts.

"No. He got all of the information he needed."

"Do you really think he voted against you?"

"A week ago, I'd have said no, but now I'm not sure." She recalled the way he'd taken to the office and how he'd worked so hard to get her a star-studded lineup for the upcoming year. "But then I messed everything up. And now I wouldn't be surprised if he didn't want any reminders of me."

Louise frowned. "I don't think he's vindictive. He struck me as a man with integrity and a solid head on his shoulders."

The dog started to squirm and so Sage set him on the floor. "I hope you're right because it's not just the magazine. It's your job and everyone else that works here."

"And no matter what, we all know that you did your best."

Sage's phone rang. In all honesty, she didn't want to talk to anyone else. She was more than willing to call it a day. But it could be the board with a decision about the magazine's future. When she checked the caller ID, it was someone totally unexpected.

CHAPTER TWENTY

TREY HAD BEEN avoiding Sage.

He didn't think he could face her again until he had everything sorted out. He'd been extremely busy since returning from France.

Ever since he'd walked away from Sage that night at the château, he'd felt as though he'd lost a piece of himself. Sure, he was upset that she'd interfered in his life and brought his father to see him. It was wrong and for a while he'd been really upset with her.

His father had followed him to the States. They'd had another talk. This time his father did most of the talking and Trey did more listening. In the end, his father told him to give Sage another chance. In the little bit of time that his father had seen them together, he said he could tell they had something special.

Trey left that meeting anxious to talk to Sage about what had just gone on between him and his father—their first meaningful conversation. But she wasn't waiting for him at home. She wasn't waiting for him. Period.

And he had no one to blame but himself. She had drawn his father back into his life out of the goodness of her heart. If there was one thing about Sage that was undeniable, it was her desire for others to be happy—even if she wasn't.

And now it was time they talked. He hoped that she would hear him out and, in the end, she'd be happy. He'd hired a team of private investigators to work through the information his hacker friends had uncovered about Elsa's dealings. And he now had incriminating proof that Elsa had stolen Sage's legacy.

And with the board meeting concluded and the official vote taken, Trey jumped in his sleek black sports car and raced across town to the headquarters of *QTR Magazine*. He maneuvered the car through the parking lot. Just as a black town car pulled out from in front of the building, he slipped his car into the vacant spot.

Not so long ago, he would have thought of this as his father's building, but now when he looked at the building, he thought of it as Sage's domain. She'd done miracles with this magazine. He was proud of her.

He rushed to the glass doors and, once inside the lobby, he came to a stop. There was Louise and Happy. He glanced around for Sage, but she was nowhere in sight.

Arf! Arf!

Trey said hi to Louise and then knelt down to pet Happy. Even though the dog was cute, he never would have considered keeping him if it weren't for Sage's fondness for Happy. Keeping a dog was a life-changing event for him. It meant scheduling his life around someone else—putting Happy's needs ahead of Trey's hectic schedule. He wouldn't do something like that for just anyone. But he had to admit he'd grown quite attached to the dog and the woman who'd convinced him to keep Happy.

Trey lifted his head to Louise. "Is Sage in her office?"

"No. She just left."

He straightened. "Left?"

Louise nodded.

Trey felt as though the rug had been pulled out from under him. He thought this was his chance to fix everything and now she'd taken off in the middle of a workday. Was she that upset with him?

Louise looked at him. "Are you just going to stand there?"

"What do you want me to do?"

"I want you to…" She glanced down at the file folder in her hand. When her gaze met his again there was a twinkle in her eyes as though she had all the answers to the world's problems. "Do you remember when you said that you would owe me a favor for watching Happy while you were in France?"

He clearly remembered. And he knew one day that favor was going to cost him dearly. It appeared that day had arrived. "I remember."

"I need you to take this file to Sage. I forgot to give it to her before she left."

His gaze lowered to the thin file folder. "Surely it can't be that important."

"She needs it for her meeting in New York."

"New York?" No wonder Sage appeared a bit on edge. He thought she was angry with the way he'd reacted over the reconciliation with his father. But she'd had other more important matters on her mind. "She's going to face Elsa, isn't she?"

"I can't really say. She swore me to silence."

That told him everything he needed to know. "Give me the file." It was the excuse he needed to speak to her and try to convince her to forgive him so he could accompany her on this trip. "I'll see that she gets it."

"I was really hoping you'd say that. And if you don't make it back for a while, no worries—Happy will be fine with me."

"You mean you'll spoil him some more."

Arf!

"Like I said, we've got this. Just make sure Sage is all right." She held out the folder to him.

He accepted it. "I will, if she lets me."

"You can be persuasive. After all, you talked her into hiring you, didn't you? Flash her that million-dollar smile, and if that doesn't work, grovel."

"Grovel?" He shook his head. He wasn't one that was used to groveling. But when he thought of living his life without Sage in it, groveling didn't seem like such a bad option. "I'll do whatever it takes." He rushed to the door and then paused to turn back. "Thank you."

"What are you thanking me for? You're the one doing me a favor." She winked at him.

"You're the best."

"Stop with the flattery and get going. You don't want to miss her."

He took off out the door. Thankfully he'd left his car right in front of the building in the no-parking zone. Sometimes rules had to be broken, especially when you realize what an idiot you've been.

He stopped next to his car and searched the parking area for the black town car that had pulled out just as he'd arrived. He was certain it would be long gone by now, but then he spotted it waiting in a long line at the red light. Most of the time that stoplight annoyed him to no end with its long green for the main drag but its five-second green for the parking lot. Today he was thanking his lucky stars because it was just the delay he needed to catch up to Sage.

He took a side exit, avoiding the troublesome light, and followed her car onto the freeway. With the congestion on the roadway, he fell back a few cars. It was no big deal as there wasn't any way to get her to pull over here. He would just follow her to the airport where he could tell her—

A car came flying up beside him. It was a flashy red sports car. It swerved into his lane, nearly side-swiping him before it rushed on.

The sports car surge forward and then it veered to the right, cutting off a car. The car braked and started a chain reaction of collisions. Trey practically stood on his brakes to get stopped in time.

When he looked up, he saw the sports car had swerved across the five lanes of traffic. Brake lights lit up. And then the car struck the fender of Sage's car. Trey watched the accident as if it was in slow motion. The black town car spun around and another oncoming car struck the passenger side.

Trey's heart lurched into his throat.

No. No. No. This can't be happening.

She just has to be okay. Please, let her be okay.

By now traffic had ground to a halt in all the lanes. Trey shut down his car and jumped out. He wasn't the only one. Others were getting out to help the passengers in the now-wrecked cars. But the red sports car was nowhere to be found. It must have slipped away on the off-ramp.

He ran toward Sage's car. The driver stepped out. He grimaced as he rubbed his neck.

Trey kept moving until he was next to Sage's door. He eased it open and found her sitting there with her head lulled off to the side and her eyes closed. A trickle of blood trailed down the side of her face.

Trey's chest tightened. This couldn't be happening. It just couldn't be too late to tell her that he was sorry. That he loved her. And he would do whatever it took to make her happy.

"Sage?" No response. "Sage, please open your eyes."

The driver moved around the car to stand next to Trey. "How is she?"

"I… I don't know." The breath caught in his lungs. He needed to see if she had a pulse. He reached out and placed a finger on the side of her neck. Her skin was warm and…there was a pulse. The pent-up breath whooshed from his lungs. "She's alive."

"I called 911. The paramedics are stuck in traffic."

Trey turned back to Sage. "Don't worry. I'm not going anywhere." He gently traced his finger down over her cheek. "I'm so sorry. That's what I came to tell you. And that I love you. I love you so much. Please be all right."

He leaned forward and pressed his lips ever so lightly to hers.

When he pulled back, he noticed her eyes start to open. He reached for her hand and took it in his own. "That's it. Come back to me."

Sage's eyes opened wide. She glanced around until her gaze settled on him. "You love me?"

"You heard that?"

She smiled and nodded. "Just tell me that it wasn't a dream."

"It's definitely not a dream." He stared deep into her blue eyes. "I love you, Sage. With all my heart. I'm just sorry that it took me so long to figure it all out."

"Why did you leave me at the château? Why couldn't we have figured it out together?"

"Because you kept talking about everything being perfect. That's a lot of pressure to put on a person—especially someone like me. I didn't think I could give you a perfect family—in fact, I knew it."

"I'm sorry. I didn't realize the pressure I was putting on you. I was so excited about what we could have together that I didn't think about how your past would color your view of the future."

"And I let the past get in the way of my future—of our future. But thanks to you, my father and I are talking. I'm learning that everything in the past wasn't black and white. I think the truth is somewhere in the shades of gray."

Sage smiled. "I'm so glad to hear that you two are talking."

"I never thought I'd say this, but I am, too."

She squeezed his hand. "I've had time to think about us. And I don't need a perfect family. All I need is you. I love you." She leaned into him and pressed her lips to his. A kiss had never tasted quite so sweet.

When she pulled back, she pressed a hand to her injured forehead. "What happened?"

"You were in an accident. Don't you remember?"

It took her a second and then she nodded. "I remember some of it."

She started to move around, but the seat belt was still holding her in place.

"Hey, you need to stay where you are until the paramedics get here." He didn't want her to hurt herself further.

"Why? I'm fine." She released the seat belt.

"You have blood on your face. You aren't fine."

"It's just a little cut."

"I'd rather hear an experienced medical professional tell me that."

She smiled at him as the paramedics entered the freeway via the exit ramp. "I never knew you were so protective."

"Only about those I love."

Sage got to her feet. "See. I'm fine."

"You're still going to the hospital to be checked out. Do you hear me?"

"But I need to get to New York. My investigator has important information about Elsa."

"While you get checked out, your investigator and my investigators can put their information together and see if it's enough to take to the police."

Her eyes widened. "You had people looking into Elsa even after our blowup over your father?"

"I never stopped. And I have some other news for you."

"Is it about the future of the magazine?" The smile slipped from her face.

"It is. The board voted unanimously for you."

"They did?" She threw her arms around his neck. "If this is a dream, don't wake me up."

"It's not a dream. I love you and everything is going to work out as long as we're together."

He lowered his head and claimed her lips with his own.

CHAPTER TWENTY-ONE

ELSA STOOD IN front of the gold leaf mirror.

"Beautiful as always." She smiled at her reflection.

Her latest facelift had done wonders to erase the years. Perhaps the doctor had been a bit zealous with how much skin he retracted as her eyes were a little off, but he assured her that she'd look like herself in no time.

The doors to her office burst open. She spun around. A distinct frown pulled at her very tight skin. "What are you doing here?"

Sage stood in the doorway with a smile on her face. For a moment, she didn't say anything. A sickening feeling took hold of Elsa's stomach. It was just like her nightmares. But that couldn't be. She'd worked so hard to keep the truth from Sage.

"It's over, Elsa." Sage stepped into her office.

"I... I don't know what you're talking about." There was no way Sage knew the truth. She was lying. "And if you don't get out of here, I'm calling security. In fact, I'm calling them right now."

As Elsa picked up the phone, Sage said, "There's no need to call them. I have the police with me."

At that moment, two New York City uniformed officers stepped up behind Sage. Elsa took a step back. This couldn't be happening. She refused to lose everything.

"You all need to go," Elsa said as though it would make it so.

"The only one leaving here is you. In handcuffs." Sage was no longer smiling. There was a very serious look on her face. "We've just handed over all of the proof the district attorney needs to prosecute you for fraud, embezzlement and a few other charges. And when they are done with you, the SEC wants their turn to try you for manipulating the company stock price. And don't worry, your buddies at the investment firm are getting their own set of bright shiny handcuffs." A big smile came over her face.

Quentin Thomas Rousseau III stepped up next to Sage. "Didn't you forget something?"

Sage turned to him. "Did I? That's a lot of charges to remember."

He nodded. "Would you like me to say it?"

"Sure."

"Stop." Elsa's stomach lurched. She didn't know which made her sicker, the pending charges or their sickening sweet act. "How did you figure it out?"

Sage lifted her chin and leveled her shoulders. "I took a page out of your book. I hired the best private investigator after I found him snooping through my office."

Elsa's gaze narrowed. "You hired Hunter?"

Sage's smile broadened. "I did. I guess you could say he was acting as a double agent."

Quentin spoke up. "Now what was I about to say?"

Sage elbowed him. "You know, what happens to Elsa after the SEC."

"That's right. Once the SEC is done with you, the IRS wants their turn at you. It appears that you've been hiding assets."

"How could I have forgotten that one?" Sage turned to Elsa. "Looks like you're in a mess of trouble. I just hope you didn't mess up my house too much. That's right. The house is coming back to me now that a copy of the original will has been located."

As the officer placed the cuffs on Elsa's wrists, the reality of the situation sunk in. Elsa glared at her stepdaughter. "Your father always loved you best. He never paid attention to what I needed. It was always Sage this and Sage that. He was never worried about me. I had to take what I deserved."

The officer started to read her rights to her. Elsa took one last look around her precious office. And then her gaze landed on Sage and Quentin as they shared a tender look.

"You will never win," Elsa said as she was led toward the door.

"We already did." Sage leaned over and kissed Quentin.

EPILOGUE

Six months later...

IT WAS FINALLY HAPPENING.

Trey was at last going to have the family that he'd always wanted—and wondered if he deserved.

Sage had taught him to forgive himself—and his father. He glanced off to the side to find his father sitting in the back row of their small wedding. If it wasn't for Sage, he didn't think he would have ever been able to open his heart up to his father. He never would have known the truth—his father hadn't left voluntarily. His mother had pushed him away because she wasn't able to share him with his work. She was an overly insecure person. But his mother had never shared that information with Trey. She'd only said his father had chosen his work over them.

With his father permanently retired, the future of *QTR* was now Trey's responsibility—and Sage's. Not only were they merging their hearts and lives, but they also were merging their companies. They were going to be a dynamic duo, at work and at home.

Trey returned his attention to his almost-wife

as Sage repeated her wedding vows. He stared into her eyes, seeing his future. He couldn't imagine choosing his work over her. Nor could he imagine her issuing an ultimatum. Sage enjoyed her work as much as he did. But they both enjoyed their time together. Sometimes it was a balancing act. Some days work won out. But other times, they'd slip away for some alone time—which they would do shortly for their month-long honeymoon.

"You may kiss your bride," the minister said.

Arf! Arf!

They both looked down at Happy, who sat between them wearing his little black bow tie. His tail rapidly swished back and forth. Was it Trey's imagination or was the dog smiling at them?

Trey gave himself a mental shake. He lifted his gaze until it met his wife's. They both leaned in close and he pressed his lips to hers. Her kiss excited him just as much now as it had the very first time that they'd kissed. There was definitely something magical about Sage. And he was so lucky to have her next to him for life.

They turned to the couple dozen people that they'd invited to the small, intimate affair. Standing and clapping were all the people that held a special place in their hearts.

Sage leaned closer to Trey. "Is that your father in the back row?"

"It is. I told him if he didn't have anything planned that he could stop by."

"Really?" Sage sent him an astonished look.

"What? I thought you'd be happy."

"I'm happy he's here, but the way you invited him, it was like asking him over to watch a football game. I would have sent him an invitation if you'd have mentioned that you changed your mind. Now what's he going to think? And sitting in the back row of all places."

Trey turned to his bride and cupped her face. "He's going to think I'm the luckiest man in the world. And he has just gained the most beautiful and kindhearted daughter-in-law. Now give me a kiss."

She lifted up on her tiptoes and he met her halfway. But the kiss was much too short as Sage pulled away. He sent her a puzzled look.

"You'll get more later," she said. "We have guests."

"Promise?"

"I do."

He grinned. He'd never been happier in his life. Something told him with Sage by his side that life was just going to get sweeter.

Outside the church, he held Happy in his arms while Sage gathered the single ladies around. She tossed her bridal bouquet. It tumbled through the air and landed in Louise's hands. The woman's face lit up with a big smile.

Sage leaned into her husband's side. "Looks like there's going to be another wedding."

"What makes you think that?"

"Watch."

As the crowd scattered, Ralph from the accounting department approached Louise. He took her in his arms. She smiled up at him and they kissed.

"I think you're right, Mrs. Rousseau."

Sage smiled up at him. "You keep talking like that and we're going to have a very happy marriage."

Arf! Arf!

He turned to Happy. "You're supposed to be on my side. Us guys, we need to stick together."

Sage laughed and it was the best thing Trey had ever heard. He planned to keep her laughing the rest of their days.

* * * * *

Get 4 FREE REWARDS!

We'll send you 2 FREE Books plus 2 FREE Mystery Gifts.

FREE
Value Over
$20

Both the **Romance** and **Suspense** collections feature compelling novels written by many of today's best-selling authors.

YES! Please send me 2 FREE novels from the Essential Romance or Essential Suspense Collection and my 2 FREE gifts (gifts are worth about $10 retail). After receiving them, if I don't wish to receive any more books, I can return the shipping statement marked "cancel." If I don't cancel, I will receive 4 brand-new novels every month and be billed just $6.74 each in the U.S. or $7.24 each in Canada. That's a savings of at least 16% off the cover price. It's quite a bargain! Shipping and handling is just 50¢ per book in the U.S. and 75¢ per book in Canada*. I understand that accepting the 2 free books and gifts places me under no obligation to buy anything. I can always return a shipment and cancel at any time. The free books and gifts are mine to keep no matter what I decide.

Choose one: ☐ **Essential Romance**
(194/394 MDN GMY7)

☐ **Essential Suspense**
(191/391 MDN GMY7)

Name (please print)

Address   Apt. #

City   State/Province   Zip/Postal Code

Mail to the **Reader Service:**
IN U.S.A.: P.O. Box 1341, Buffalo, NY 14240-8531
IN CANADA: P.O. Box 603, Fort Erie, Ontario L2A 5X3

Want to try two free books from another series? Call 1-800-873-8635 or visit www.ReaderService.com.

*Terms and prices subject to change without notice. Prices do not include applicable taxes. Sales tax applicable in NY. Canadian residents will be charged applicable taxes. Offer not valid in Quebec. This offer is limited to one order per household. Books received may not be as shown. Not valid for current subscribers to the Essential Romance or Essential Suspense Collection. All orders subject to approval. Credit or debit balances in a customer's account(s) may be offset by any other outstanding balance owed by or to the customer. Please allow 4 to 6 weeks for delivery. Offer available while quantities last.

Your Privacy—The Reader Service is committed to protecting your privacy. Our Privacy Policy is available online at www.ReaderService.com or upon request from the Reader Service. We make a portion of our mailing list available to reputable third parties that offer products we believe may interest you. If you prefer that we not exchange your name with third parties, or if you wish to clarify or modify your communication preferences, please visit us at www.ReaderService.com/consumerchoice or write to us at Reader Service Preference Service, P.O. Box 9062, Buffalo, NY 14240-9062. Include your complete name and address.

STRS18

READERSERVICE.COM

Manage your account online!

- Review your order history
- Manage your payments
- Update your address

*We've designed the
Reader Service website
just for you.*

Enjoy all the features!

- Discover new series available to you, and read excerpts from any series.
- Respond to mailings and special monthly offers.
- Browse the Bonus Bucks catalog and online-only exculsives.
- Share your feedback.

Visit us at:
ReaderService.com

RS16R